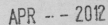

BORN TO FLY

BORN TO FLY

MICHAEL FERRARI

A YEARLING BOOK

All rights reserved. Published in the United States by Yearling, an imprint of Random House Children's Books, a division of Random House, Inc., New York. Originally published in hardcover in the United States by Delacorte Press, an imprint of Random House Children's Books, a division of Random House, Inc., New York, in 2009.

Yearling and the jumping horse design are registered trademarks of Random House, Inc.

Visit us on the Web! www.randomhouse.com/kids

Educators and librarians, for a variety of teaching tools, visit us at
www.randomhouse.com/teachers

The Library of Congress has cataloged the hardcover edition of this work as follows:
Ferrari, Michael (Michael J.)
Born to fly / Michael Ferrari. — 1st ed.
p. cm.
Summary: In 1942, an eleven-year-old girl who longs to be a pilot and her family try to manage their lives in Rhode Island when the father goes to fight in World War II.
ISBN 978-0-385-73715-9 (trade) — ISBN 978-0-385-90649-4 (lib. bdg.)
ISBN 978-0-375-89096-3 (ebook)
[1. Flight—Fiction. 2. Airplanes—Fiction. 3. Family life—Rhode Island—Fiction.
4. Friendship—Fiction. 5. Sex role—Fiction. 6. World War, 1939–1945—Fiction. 7. Rhode Island—History—20th century—Fiction.] I. Title.
PZ7.F3644Bo 2009
[Fic]—dc22
2008035664

ISBN 978-0-375-84607-6 (pbk.)

Printed in the United States of America

10 9 8 7 6 5 4 3

First Yearling Edition
2011

For my daughters,
Clarissa and Eva

ACKNOWLEDGMENTS

Special thanks to:

My parents and family, for years of encouragement and confidence in me, especially when I lacked it in myself;

My friends and fellow writers Karol Silverstein, Paula Yoo, Greg Neri, and Leigh Purtill, who know how special this is;

And especially to my wife, Pattie, who makes it all worthwhile.

This book was made possible in part by a grant from the Society of Children's Book Writers and Illustrators.

CHAPTER 1

Just 'cause I was a girl in 1941, don't think I was some sissy. Shoot, I saw stuff that would've made that bully Farley Peck pee right through his pants. Like summer, the year before. That's when me and my best friend Wendy saw the Genny, the giant man-eating sea serpent that lived in Geneseo Bay. Except Wendy didn't get a good look like I did. To tell you the truth, I don't think she really saw anything, she just said she did to back me up. That's what friends do. But then Wendy's dad got a job building roads, or houses, or something with the Work Projects Administration, and they moved to Wisconsin. It didn't really matter, because no one believed me anyway. I was always seeing stuff that no one else did. Mom thought I probably just needed glasses, but my dad said it was because I had "imagination." Once, when I was two, they found me way up on the roof of our barn. Dad said I must have flown up there. That's how I got my name.

"What do you think, Bird?"

"This is the best birthday present ever, Dad."

We were flying above the clouds in Mr. Watson's yellow Piper. I guided the small propeller plane so that it moved through the air just like an eagle. Seeing me in my World War One pilot's skullcap and goggles and my Huck Finn dungarees, you would've never guessed that someone with a neat name like Bird McGill was actually just an eleven-year-old girl. But I was. I worked the controls carefully, scanning the skies for bogies at twelve o'clock.

"She's no Warhawk, but she sure beats that puddle jumper we had last year," Dad told me.

My dad was a mechanic, the best one around. He could fix just about anything, but his favorite things were airplanes. He had rebuilt Mr. Watson's airplane carburetor last month.

"Mr. Watson says we can take her up anytime," Dad said.

This wasn't the first time I'd been up in a plane. Dad had taken me up plenty of times. My big sister Margaret was afraid to go and my little brother Alvin was still too young. Mom flew with us sometimes, but she didn't like it like I did. Plus, when Mom wasn't around and it was just the two of us, Dad would let me take the controls. I knew just about all there was to know about flying. You have to watch your airspeed and your altimeter (that's what tells you how high you are). You've got to know how to ride your rudder, adjust your trim and throttle, and know just how much flaps to use when taking off and landing. My favorite airplane was the P-40 Warhawk. It was the most beautiful thing I'd ever seen. Someday, I was gonna fly one.

See, every airplane needs wings and a tail. The wings need flaps, and the tail needs a rudder. And it's a good idea to have wheels, if you ever hope to land and take off again. But you can hardly call it an airplane if it doesn't look like it was born to fly. An airplane can only fly as good as it looks. My dad said it's like falling in love. If one look at the plane doesn't make you want to shoot up into the clouds, the plane's hardly worth talking about.

Down below us was Geneseo, the town where we lived. It's in the state of Rhode Island. Funny thing is, Rhode Island isn't an island at all. An island has water on all sides, like Hawaii or Treasure Island. But we only had water on one side. We lived near the ocean, but thanks to the bay, which hooked around like a big arm, we could swim and fish and the water never got too rough, like it did farther out in the Atlantic Ocean.

My dad's name was Peter. That was what Mom called him when she was scared or mad, or didn't want him to let me do something that she thought was too dangerous or unladylike (like flying an airplane). My dad was handsome, with strong arms and a big, easy smile. I liked the way he looked at me when I was flying. Like he was proud.

When you're flying and you look down, everything looks different. All the stuff you thought was so big, or scary, is just small. Underneath us, Geneseo was laid out like a map, with Main Street dividing the town in half. On the north side were the bay, the airfield, our house, and the Widow Gorman's farm. On the other side were nine or ten clusters of houses in little rows. Main Street was crooked, and from up here it looked like a lazy snake. It was lined with two wavy rows of maple trees planted by Ruth Geneseo more than two hundred years ago to welcome her husband home from the Indian Wars. The story goes, Ruth couldn't see too well, so the trees weren't exactly in a straight line. But her husband, Wilford, thought they were the most beautiful things he'd ever seen. He built a hotel at the end of the road so that everyone would get to walk right between the two rows of trees whenever they came to town. To my left I saw the white roof of the courthouse, then a dull red box that must have been the school, and finally the pointy spire of the church. Below my right wing I could even see two men fishing from a rowboat in the bay, far below.

"I bet that's Father Krauss trying to catch the Genny," I blurted out, but then caught myself. See, I wasn't supposed to talk about the Genny. "Sorry."

But Dad just smiled, like he didn't hear. "So you're really eleven today, huh? That's pretty old."

"I can finally reach all the pedals," I told him.

4

"Why, I bet in another year you'll be ready to land this thing."

"Another year?"

"Here. You better let me line up our approach. You've got a birthday party to get to."

I reluctantly handed over the controls so that Dad could turn the plane around toward Mr. Watson's grass airstrip.

"I'll die if I have to wait another year," I said under my breath.

"What's that?"

"It's just . . . A year is practically forever."

"I see." Dad looked at me, the same way he looked at Mom when she was bugging him to take her to see *her* mom, Grandma Birch, in Buffalo. "Well, a year is too long to stare at that sad face. I guess you're gonna have to land this thing."

"Really?" I screamed.

He handed back the controls and cautioned me, "Remember, landing's the toughest part of flying."

"I know."

At first I couldn't tell if I was more excited or scared. Then Dad winked at me and said, "Relax. I know you can do it."

That was it. I got embarrassed by all his faith in me and so, like always, I rose to meet his expectations. I took the controls. Pulled back on the throttle. Leveled off for final approach. It was obvious. I was a natural. Making my descent like an old pro! We laughed and smiled. I checked my instruments. Everything looked okay.

Then suddenly the engine hit an air pocket and hiccupped.

"Easy," Dad said calmly. "Remember, don't choke it."

Right. Don't choke it. That's something you never want to do on approach. But I panicked and goosed the throttle. The engine sputtered and gasped like a sick duck. I wrestled with the mixture of fuel and air. Suddenly it was the scariest sound any pilot ever heard: complete silence. The engine stalled.

"Dad!"

My dad grabbed the controls—but the plane was dropping like a rock, the wind whistling past the cockpit windows.

"Hold on!" Dad yelled.

The panic in his voice was what really scared me. He dipped the nose. I could hear the rivets of the fuselage rattle with the increased strain. The rushing wind feathered the propeller like a pinwheel. I couldn't believe this was happening. And it was all my fault! But Dad didn't seem to be thinking about that kind of stuff. He was focused on what he had to do to fix the problem. The whole plane was shaking like crazy and yet somehow he carefully set the throttle. Picked his moment. Primed the engine. Then jumped the starter.

C-c-coughhh.

I covered my eyes and prayed.

It started! The two of us looked at each other and screamed in triumph.

6

Moments later, I stared in awe as my dad gently landed the plane beside Mr. Watson's cornfield like nothing had happened. We taxied to a stop, and at last Dad let out a big sigh.

I was still shaking and stuttering, trying to apologize. "I'm so sorry, Dad. I shouldn't have goosed the throttle."

He smiled, wiping the sweat from his brow, and steadied my hand. "It's okay, Bird. I wouldn't let you miss your own party, would I?"

By the time afternoon rolled around, the December skies had gone back to cloudy gray. Sitting on the roof of our barn, I had a bird's-eye view of our backyard picnic table and the remnants of my disastrous unattended birthday party—unused hats, clean paper plates, unopened party favors. Mom had made me hand out invitations to all the girls in my class. Not a single one came. They weren't my friends or anything, but still, when you're ten years old, you must really despise someone to turn down free cake and ice cream. I bet Minnie Lashley had told them all not to come. I'd kind of "forgotten" to give Minnie an invitation. Why did Wendy's stupid dad have to move her away? This was quickly turning into the worst birthday ever. While I peeled splinters off the roof shingles, my kid brother Alvin paced anxiously below.

"Come on, Bird. Don't you want any birthday cake?" Alvin was only four but he had a voice like Louis Armstrong. It was so deep and hoarse, like he woke up gargling a bullfrog. You'd never believe it could come out of such a small person.

"You can have it," I told him.

"But Mom said I can't, until you have some," he countered.

My sister Margaret slammed the back door and marched out of the house grumbling to herself.

"I'm not her mother. I'm sixteen, you know?" she hollered back at Mom.

She had to point out that she was sixteen a million times a day. As if anybody cared. Margaret dragged Dad out from under the chopped fuselage of an old biplane that had been parked at the side of our house for forever.

"Dad, Bird's on the roof again." Margaret led him toward the barn, all the time fussing with her hair. Lately that was how she spent most of her time—because of boys. How stupid.

"Do you have any idea how perfectly impossible it is to scare up a date in this town?" she went on. "Especially when your kid sister thinks she's the Red Baron?"

Dad chuckled.

"I'm not kidding, Dad. It's embarrassing."

Embarrassing? She spent an hour every morning stuffing socks in her bra and *I* was embarrassing?

"I'll talk to her," Dad said.

As they crossed the backyard, Mom threw the kitchen window open. She was more serious than Dad was about most things. And she wasn't like a lot of the other moms in town. Sometimes it was almost like she wasn't happy being a mom. Which didn't make sense, because then why did she become one?

She barked over the sounds of the Glenn Miller Orchestra coming from the radio, "Tell her the candles are melting."

"Roger," Dad called out.

Dad and Margaret joined Alvin by the barn below me.

"She's just pouting 'cause no one came to her stupid party," Margaret said.

"Shut up," I told her, and tried to hit her with a pebble.

"Margaret. Take Alvin inside," Dad said.

Margaret snatched Alvin's hand. It must have been sticky, as usual.

"What *is* that?" she shrieked.

Alvin licked his fingers to check.

"Chocolate, I think."

She groaned and dragged him away.

Dad climbed the ladder to the roof. As he reached the top, a crop duster made a low pass on its way to our neighbor Mrs. Gorman's cornfield.

"Staggerwing?"

"Uh-uh," I told him. "Tiger Moth."

"By gosh, you're right."

I knew he was just playing dumb, but it was sort of a routine we had. Like Abbott and Costello.

Dad sat down beside me. "Mom said you haven't eaten all day."

"If I keep eating, I'll end up like Margaret. You know . . ." I cupped my hands below my chest, like boobs.

He smiled. "That's the nature of things. Little girls become women, boys become men."

"Margaret said women can't be fighter pilots," I told him. "So I decided I'm not gonna be a woman."

"Hmm. I see."

We sat there quietly, just watching the crop duster. It seemed like a long time, but Dad was a lot better than me at this. He waited me out. Eventually I couldn't stand it.

"Aren't you gonna make me?" I asked.

"Make you what?"

"Eat."

"Nope. You're eleven. You're old enough to know when you're hungry. One thing I will tell you—" But he stopped himself. "Oh, never mind."

That was the worst, when Dad was about to say something but then changed his mind. It drove me crazy! I had to know what he was gonna say. "What?" I pleaded.

"Oh, what's the point? The only one you listen to is Margaret."

I sure didn't like the sound of that. So I moved a little closer to Dad. That was how I usually got him to spill the beans. "What do *you* think?" I asked.

"Me? Well, I've only known you eleven years, so I could be wrong, but I think you can be whatever you want to be."

"Really?" I said.

"Really. And I'm not just saying that 'cause I'm your father. You're special, Bird."

"Special." That's a code word adults use when they don't want to admit that something's not as good. Like the "special" shoes Alvin had to wear until he was three to straighten out his feet.

"I'm weird. That's why nobody came to my birthday party. No one believes I saw the Genny in the bay."

"I do," Dad said.

I nudged closer and he wrapped his arm around my shoulder.

"Know something, Dad?"

"Hmm?"

"Since Wendy moved away, you've become my best friend. Actually, you're my only friend." I could feel my chest shiver and my eyes get full, like when you have to sneeze. Only I didn't have to sneeze. I tried to hold it in, but I couldn't. All those years spent showing people I wasn't like those other sissy girls—and now this.

"Listen. You don't realize it, but there's someone out there right now, just waiting and wishing for a friend like you."

"Where?"

"Where you never thought to look," he said. My dad was smart and all, but some stuff he said didn't make any sense.

"Then how will I find them?" I asked.

"Just be yourself, and they'll find you." He looked at me in that way he had, that somehow let me know things would be okay.

That is, until my mom let out a shriek from the house. "Peter! Peter!"

We could both tell from her panicked voice that it was serious, so Dad jumped right down off the roof (which seemed, from up here, like about a hundred feet). He started for the house, not waiting for me.

"Dad?" Without him there, I was kind of scared to climb down the ladder.

Then Mom yelled again, "Peter! Hurry!"

But Dad stopped and came back for me. "Go ahead," he called out.

As soon as I saw him stay, I was no longer afraid. In fact, I felt ten feet tall. I shoved the ladder aside, and I jumped like my dad, landing on a small pile of hay. Dad didn't wait as I dusted myself off.

By the time I stumbled into our living room, Mom, Margaret, Alvin, and Dad were all huddled around the radio.

"What's the big deal?" I asked.

"*Shhh!*" ordered Margaret.

"*Shhh* yourself," I told her.

"Bird!" Dad hollered (which made me clam up quick, because Dad never yelled at me like that). I heard the announcer say:

"... *to bring you a special news bulletin. This morning, Japanese planes attacked the American military base in Pearl Harbor. . . . President Roosevelt spoke in an emergency address. . . .*"

Then the President came on: *"December 7, 1941—a date which will live in infamy—the United States of America was suddenly and deliberately attacked by naval and air forces of the Empire of Japan. . . . With confidence in our armed forces, with the unbounding determination of our people, we will gain the inevitable triumph, so help us God."*

As the report continued, I watched Mom hold Alvin a little tighter. Dad wrapped his arm around Mom's shoulder. But it was the look of worry on his face that frightened me the most.

On the coffee table was my birthday cake. Most of the candles and now *Bird* and the number eleven were one messy pink swirl of wax and frosting. I knelt down, lit the one remaining candle, took a big breath, and closed my eyes.

And all of a sudden I found myself wishing I was still ten.

CHAPTER

2

February in Rhode Island is cold and snowy like nobody's business. I'm not sure what that means exactly, but it's what Dad said every winter after the first snowstorm hit. We were at the train station all the way up in Providence, the capital of Rhode Island. It was a big city compared to Geneseo. I had only been to Providence once before, when we drove Mr. Ramponi to pick up his wife when she finally came over from Italy. But that was a happy trip to the train station. Trips like that usually are, when you're picking someone up. It's not the same when you're dropping someone off. Especially if that someone is your dad.

Just about everyone at the station seemed sad. The snow sprinkled over the families saying goodbye on the platform like giant grains of rice at one of Father Krauss's weddings. The conductor whistled and the soldiers and sailors reluctantly grabbed their duffel bags, kissed goodbye, and filed on board.

Dad set Alvin down and hugged Margaret. Mom just stared like a statue. I was standing apart from the family. I didn't understand why everyone was just letting this happen. No one else seemed to care. Why didn't Mom *make* Dad stay?

"Stop pouting, Bird," Mom scolded me. She'd get mad whenever Dad tried to comfort me. "Don't encourage her," she said.

"Come on, Bird," Dad cooed, like a big father pigeon before he goes off to find worms.

But I kept a stiff upper lip. I'd made up my mind an hour before, I wasn't gonna let him see me cry.

"I was saving this for your next birthday." Dad pulled out a dog-eared pilot's manual. "I won it from a guy in boot camp."

My eyes went wide as I read the worn cover: *The Curtiss P-40 Warhawk*. "That's the same one the Flying Tigers used!"

"The very same." Dad huddled down close to me. "And you know what it says in there?"

I shook my head.

"Anyone who memorizes this book can fly a Warhawk. Anyone."

I took it and wrapped my arms around his neck, crying into the snowflakes on his shoulder.

"But who's going to believe me now?" I asked.

He lifted my chin with his finger. "The only one who needs to. You."

The pushy conductor whistled a second time and the train wheels started to screech and turn. Maybe if I held tight enough, Dad would miss his train? But Dad pulled me off, turned to Mom, and said, "I'll write to let you know when I get leave."

He hugged Mom real tight. Then he pulled his dog tags from inside his shirt and showed her his wedding ring safely looped onto the chain.

"You know I love you," she told him.

"I was counting on it," he said in her ear.

Then they kissed, the way I had never seen them kiss before—a really long, sad goodbye.

Without my realizing it, my two mittened hands found their way into Margaret's and Alvin's, and we all held tight. A cloud of steam swirled around, concealing our mother and father. We stood there for what seemed like forever.

When the steam cleared, Dad and the train were gone.

CHAPTER 3

As I lay in my bed throwing bits of bubble gum at a newspaper cartoon on my wall of that stupid Jap who started the war, Emperor Hirohito, all I could think about was how the two months Dad had been gone felt like two years.

Mom knocked on our bedroom door. When she popped her head in a few seconds later, I almost pegged her with a wad of gum.

"Come on, you two," she said. "Can't miss the first day of spring."

Margaret ignored her and rolled over onto the curlers she had in her hair. She groaned, half asleep.

I hated having to share a room with her. Sometimes, when Alvin had a nightmare, I got to sleep in his room (to keep the monsters out).

I kept up my Hirohito target practice, even getting one shot right between the eyes, until something froze me dead in my tracks. It was a beautiful noise, a distant hum that was somehow strangely familiar, like a billion bumblebees swarming home to the hive. I flew out of bed and peeled the blackout shade from the window. Ever since the war started we'd had to keep our windows covered all night in case enemy planes came across the Atlantic looking for something to bomb.

"Margaret, look!"

She scrambled to the window. "What? What is it?"

I pointed to the distant sky. "Airplanes." Approaching from the airfield, five planes flew low in formation. "A whole squadron," I told her.

Margaret sighed, unimpressed, then marched out of the room. "Mother. When am I getting my own room?"

I ignored her. She didn't know what she was missing.

Our house was a few miles from town and half a dozen acres from anyone or anything. It was a drafty yellow farmhouse that creaked like an old rocking chair whenever the wind blew. I think the reason Dad liked it was that it was the only house near Mr. Watson's airfield. After Dad realized he and Mom couldn't make anything grow (except some weird-shaped pumpkins in the garden), he sold part of our field to the Army. I think he had it in his mind all along to use our barn to fix up airplanes.

When I finally dragged myself downstairs to the kitchen, Alvin was gulping down the last of his milk. He and I watched as Mom struggled with our temperamental furnace "grate."

"Daddy just kicks it," Alvin told her.

I shushed him. I tried not to bring up Dad too much around Mom, ever since I heard her crying in her room one night after Dad left.

Mom got a sad look on her face and even little Alvin realized he had said the wrong thing. Mom got up and she let her frustration out with a good swift kick. And what do you know, the old grate actually coughed up some heat.

"That's showing it who's boss," Alvin said. This made Mom and me share a laugh, which didn't happen much. It was too bad, because she was really pretty when she laughed. I wished she did it more often.

"Those stupid airplanes woke me up this morning," Margaret whined as she cleaned up after breakfast.

"Father Krauss said they're turning the old airstrip into some kind of military flight school," Mom told us.

Suddenly Margaret's eyes lit up. "Airmen? Here in Geneseo?"

It figured. She was more interested in the pilots than in the planes.

I slid off my chair and grabbed my books, all the while

tugging at my itchy new outfit. Mom had insisted I wear this new dress she made. You could tell by the way the buttons didn't exactly line up with the holes that Mom wasn't the greatest seamstress.

"I told you it would fit," she said.

Fit? Couldn't she see that the sleeves were two different lengths? "You're not really gonna make me wear it?"

"You can't expect to make friends if you don't try to fit in."

"But I look like Minnie Lashley," I said.

"Minnie's a fine young lady," Mom said.

"Maybe. But she throws like a girl," I told her with disgust. See, everybody thinks girls can't throw, which isn't true, because I'm a girl and I threw better than any of the boys except Tommy Rogers. But thanks to girls like Minnie, you never want people to say you throw like a girl, take my word for it.

"That's enough, Bird. You'll wear it and like it. Now I want you to take these to the Widow Gorman." She handed me a tin of cookies. I sniffed them hungrily. I couldn't remember the last time Mom had made cookies for me.

"But I thought you couldn't stand her."

Mom seemed hurt by what I said. Like I'd made fun of her hairstyle or told somebody how old she was. Maybe she'd forgotten how much of a busybody the Widow Gorman was, always gossiping about other people's business and saying stuff she knew wasn't true? Like when she told her bridge club that Mom had trained possums to pee all over her vegetable garden just so the widow's prize tomatoes wouldn't grow big enough to win at the county fair anymore.

"It's different now with the war," Mom said as she looked out the window. "She's lost her son."

"Is that why she's got a gold star in her window?" I asked.

"Yes," she answered softly.

I took the tin from Mom and stepped up on one of our kitchen chairs. I closed my eyes and kissed the blue cloth star hanging in our window. Blue meant that Dad was gonna be okay. "For luck," I said.

Then Mom got all sniffly and pushed me out the door to school. "Get going. And none of your shortcuts or you'll be late." Mom never let us see her cry.

CHAPTER

I dropped off the tin of cookies at the Widow Gorman's. Compared to our house, hers was awfully quiet. When I got there she was just sitting on the front porch swing in the same black dress she'd been wearing for two months. Her eyes didn't even move. They just stared down at this portrait she clutched of her son, Charlie, in his white Navy uniform.

"These are from my mom," I told her.

She didn't say anything back, so I set the tin down on a nearby chair. I stared up at the gold star in her window. It wasn't as pretty as you'd think. Normally, you'd figure that gold is better than blue—but it wasn't to anyone who knew what a gold star meant. I bet the Widow Gorman would have given everything in the world to trade that gold star for a blue one, if she could. When I looked down, I noticed something wrong with her shoelace.

"Hey, your shoe's untied." I bent down and carefully tied it for her. A double knot, the way my dad had taught me. "You don't want to trip and fall, do you?" I wasn't sure, but I thought she gave me a hint of a smile. I smiled back just in case.

The land Dad sold to the Army started a couple acres south of our house, right next to the Widow Gorman's cornfield, and stretched across the ravine, from Moorewood Hill all the way to Johnson's mill. I was shortcutting across Mrs. Gorman's back field, reading my P-40 pilot's manual, when I spotted Eleanor sticking her head through the boards of a new fence.

"Hiya, Eleanor."

She didn't say anything, just kept grazing like a big old dairy cow ought to. I slipped through the fence and cut across the old grass airfield, past some sign that read NO TRESPASSING—U.S. ARMY AIR CORPS TRAINING AREA.

The sound of my new dress swishing as I walked made me sort of itch. As I got near the center of the field, my feet crossed the rim of a big white circle painted in the grass. Suddenly I heard a far-off buzzing sound approaching from behind me. It grew to a roar. As I recognized the sound, I spun around in disbelief. There, diving down at me, was the greatest fighter plane ever, a P-40 Warhawk!

"Hey!" I started jumping up and down, waving my arms.

The plane tipped its wings, like maybe the pilot was fighting to see past the oil blowing on his windshield (I had read in the manual that the plane was known for leaking oil on the cockpit). Then the P-40 dipped its nose and started bearing down like a dive-bomber. I couldn't figure out what the pilot was doing, since the runway started way at the other end of the field. Suddenly I looked at the grass under my feet, and realized: I was standing in the center of a giant bull's-eye! I was the target! I waved my arms more frantically and started to run.

The last thing I saw before the Warhawk flew over was a large white bomb plummeting toward me. Running at full speed, I hit the dirt facedown as the payload exploded all around me.

I woke up in a cloud of white. Was I dead? I lifted my head to see my new dress covered with a fine white powder. Somehow I had survived the blast.

The P-40 pulled out and disappeared into the clouds. I dusted myself off and coughed up some of the white dust. I tasted it. It was *flour*. Then I remembered that the manual mentioned that they used flour bombs to train the dive-bombers. I looked over at the bull's-eye. Not bad, but this pilot was off by about ten feet.

CHAPTER

5

Like they did every morning before the bell rang, all the kids from town were screaming and carrying on as if these were the last ten minutes of freedom they were ever gonna get. Laughing at dirty jokes they didn't understand, using ponytails for the only thing they're good for (pulling), and checking to see whose mom made the worst lunch. This was my world in the yard outside Wilford Geneseo Grammar School. It was a small, four-room, red-brick building, where nine months of the year they bored us to death with decimals, times tables, and made-up spelling rules (that weren't really rules because there was always some exception). It was probably the pressure of all those silly rules that drove kids to bet their allowance that Bill Shabbing wouldn't eat the dead sea slug we found under the teeter-totter two days ago. So in the middle of all the chasing, ponytail pulling, and sea slug eating, even though I was caked with flour and dirt, no one noticed me sneaking in the utility door.

I turned down the hall and spotted Farley Peck and his green-toothed toady Raymond at the drinking fountain, playing keep-away with little Timmy Spencer's lunch bag. Farley'd had to do the second grade over again, so he was older and bigger than all us other fifth graders. He was even bigger than most of the sixth graders. His hair was always dirty and hanging in his eyes, like he was two months overdue for a haircut. And he stuttered sometimes when he talked, which made some kids laugh (you couldn't help it, but that gave Farley plenty of excuses to start fights). He'd pick fights with anyone. Even girls. Especially ones who wanted to be fighter pilots.

Unfortunately, Farley and Raymond were standing between me and the girls' room. When I'd had Wendy it was a little safer. At least there were two of us. Now it was just me.

Raymond held Timmy while Farley dumped out the kid's lunch bag and found a Hershey bar.

"Chocolate?" Farley said.

"Number one on the ration list," said Raymond. Because of the war, everything was running out: metal, rubber, meat, eggs. So everything had to be rationed. The government passed out coupons you had to use when you wanted to buy something that was being rationed.

"What if the Japs got hold of this?" Farley asked him. "We'll have to c-c-confus . . . confusk . . ."

"Confiscate it?" Timmy piped up helpfully.

"Steal it," Farley barked back as he took a big bite out of the chocolate bar.

Then Raymond discovered a folded letter in Timmy's pocket. "What's this? A love letter?"

Timmy lunged to retrieve it. "Give me that!"

"Why should I?" Raymond said.

"It's from my father," Timmy cried.

Suddenly Farley snatched the letter away from Raymond. I figured now was the time to make my move to try and sneak past.

"What gives?" Raymond said.

Farley threw the letter back to Timmy.

"You turning sappy?" Raymond said, without thinking (as usual).

That wasn't the kind of thing you said to Farley. Raymond quickly tried to distract him—and that was when he noticed me. "Hey, Farley. Look what the dog dragged in."

"It's 'cat,'" I said. "Look what the *cat* dragged in." I should have kept my mouth shut but I couldn't help correcting such dim-witted tormentors. Even bullies should have standards.

Farley jumped at the opportunity and cut me off. "Is that you under there, Birdbrain? In a d-d-dress?"

I knew this was gonna happen the moment I put the thing on.

"Maybe she's getting married?" Raymond said.

I tried to pass, but Farley blocked my way with his grimy arm.

"Just let me by, Farley," I said.

"Be my guest," he said, stepping aside.

But as I passed, Farley swiped my P-40 manual right out of my hand.

"What's this?" he asked.

"Give me that!" I demanded.

But Farley was a good head taller than me and easily kept it out of my reach.

"You want it? Go get it." And with that, he kicked a door open and tossed the book deep into the boys' bathroom.

I hesitated while I weighed my options.

"What's the matter?" Farley said. "I thought you wanted to be a boy."

I shoved him out of my way and made a quick rush to retrieve the book. But as soon as I was inside, I heard the squeak of a chair as the two punks quickly jammed the door from the outside.

BRRRING, the morning bell rang. I slammed my shoulder against the door, fighting to free the chair, but Farley and Raymond held it fast. So I let loose with fists and feet, pounding and kicking the door.

"Farley! You jerk! Open up!"

Suddenly, a toilet in one of the stalls flushed. I realized I wasn't alone in the boys' bathroom. I pounded more frantically.

"Raymond!" Slowly, the stall door creaked open . . . and I was horrified to find myself face to face with a real live Jap—in a cowboy hat!

"Ahhh!" I screamed.

Incredibly, he screamed right back at me, "Ahhh!"

And before I realized it, I had knocked the chair free and I was racing down the hall at the speed of sound.

I skidded into my classroom, past my teacher, Mrs. Simmons, whose flabby arms were busy flapping as she wrote on the blackboard.

"Miss McGill, what did we say about running?"

Between gasps I spit out, "Mrs. Simmons! There's a big . . . with a knife and . . ."

"Good heavens, Bird, what happened to your dress?"

I looked down at my flour-covered frock. "One of our fighter planes bombed me by accident."

She gave me that *look*, like when I told everyone about the Genny. "Bird. You have to stop these ridiculous stories." Mrs. Simmons ushered me to my desk.

"But there's one of *them*, in the bathroom," I protested.

"One of whom?"

"The enemy!"

"Of course there is," Mrs. Simmons said blandly. "And that's why we wash our hands."

I plopped down in my seat as the last of my classmates filed in. There was a knock on the door and Principal Hartwig called Mrs. Simmons into the hall.

Farley sneered at me, figuring I had tattled on him. "T-t-traitor."

"Takes one to know one," I snarled back.

Farley took out his grammar book and began to stuff it down the back of his pants, in case he was gonna get paddled again. "I'll get you for this, Bird," he said.

Mrs. Simmons stepped back into the room. "Class, I want your attention."

She seemed nervous. Everyone started to quiet down. Maybe they'd found the Jap?

"We have a new classmate. His name is Ken-ji Fujita."

Everybody started muttering: "What?" "Who?" "What kind of name is that?"

Then Kenji Fujita stepped in—and all the muttering stopped dead.

I jumped to my feet and screamed. "That's him!"

Kenji Fujita was the big Jap I ran into in the bathroom. Except he wasn't very big (probably two or three inches shorter than me), and he didn't have a knife, and to tell you the truth he looked kind of startled by my outburst. Then Mr. Fujita, a lobster trapper who fished with Father Krauss and who was, up until then, the only Jap in all of Geneseo, stepped into the room with Principal Hartwig. Mr. Fujita said something in Japanese that seemed to calm Kenji.

"Bird. Sit down," Mrs. Simmons said.

Susan, the red-haired girl who sat next to me, had to tug me back down to my seat.

"I think there's an empty seat in the back, Ken-ji," Mrs. Simmons said. She pointed to the seat next to me.

Kenji scowled at the way Mrs. Simmons carefully pronounced his name. He answered her with a pretty good imitation of John Wayne. "Ma'am. My friends call me . . . Ringo."

Mr. Fujita scolded him in Japanese and Kenji pulled his cowboy hat off.

"Yes, Uncle." Kenji moped like a wounded cowpoke to the empty seat. He was too busy giving me the evil eye to notice when Farley Peck stuck his foot out.

Kenji tripped and fell face-first onto the floor. The class roared with laughter. Me too. I couldn't believe it. For once, I was on the laughing side instead of the face-on-the-floor side. Kenji jumped back to his feet, angry and ready to fight.

Mr. Fujita yelled something in Japanese.

"He started it," Kenji muttered.

Farley stood up from his seat. He towered over Kenji.

"Kenji!" Mr. Fujita locked eyes with his nephew.

Kenji lowered his fists.

"Why don't you go home to Japland?" Farley said.

"That's enough!" said Principal Hartwig. Our principal didn't say much, but when he did speak, everybody listened. Maybe that was 'cause he was in the Great War. Or maybe because he had a wooden leg. He lost his real leg

31

somewhere in France. When I was little I used to wonder what would happen if some French kid found it, but then I realized that by "lost" they just meant it got blown off by a bomb or something. It's pretty gross when you think about it.

"Kenji is our guest," Principal Hartwig said. "Now, I want you all to apologize."

We all mumbled a fake "sorry" in unison. Then Mrs. Simmons helped Kenji gather his things. I noticed that Kenji's fists were clenched so tightly, his knuckles were white. He lowered his eyes and slid into the seat next to me as his uncle left with Principal Hartwig.

"Minnie, why don't you lead us in the Pledge of Allegiance?" Mrs. Simmons said.

We all stood. Like always, Minnie Lashley showed off her dimples as she perfectly pronounced: "I pledge allegiance to the flag of the United States of America . . ."

The rest of the class joined in. I listened and watched with surprise as Kenji recited the pledge along with us, in perfect English, ". . . and to the Republic for which it stands, one nation, indivisible, with liberty and justice for all."

"Very nice, Minnie," Mrs. Simmons said. Then she told us to take our seats.

"You speak pretty good English," I said, thinking out loud.

Kenji gave me a dirty look and barked back, "So do you."

"Now open your books." Mrs. Simmons saw Kenji raise

his hand and said to me, "Bird, I think there's enough room for Ken-ji to look on with you."

"But Mrs. Simmons—"

"No buts, Miss McGill."

Kenji reluctantly scooted his chair closer to mine.

"Now I want you all thinking of a topic for your final report. It can be on anything"—the whole class's eyes lit up—"about our fine state of Rhode Island."

We all groaned in unison.

Every day the school emptied out as soon as the final bell rang at 2:30. Usually I was racing out to avoid running into bullies like Farley, but that day I was immediately surrounded by Minnie, Susan, and Libby (a curly-haired priss who'd moved here from "New Yawk" in the spring and was always afraid of "getting dirty" at recess). I got kind of nervous, because usually the only time they ever talked to me was when I was taking too long in the bathroom.

"Gosh, how did you stand it?" asked Minnie.

"I would have died," Libby said.

"Did he say anything to you?" Susan piped up.

"Not really." I shrugged, not sure exactly what they were talking about.

Libby stretched her face to make slant-eyes and buck-teeth. "How do they see through those little slits for eyes?"

"I can't believe it," Minnie gasped. "A real Jap right here in our school."

"I heard they eat their dogs for dinner," Libby said.

"Really?" I said.

"Mm-hmm." Libby nodded. "And raw octopuses, and snakes. I read it in a book or something."

"Gross," I said. I tried to imagine what kind of person could eat snakes or raw octopuses or their own pet dog.

"My dad says they're taught from when they're babies not to feel any pain," Minnie said. "If they get burned or cut their fingers, they don't feel it. They're not like regular people. They don't even believe in God."

"*Shhh!*" Susan covered her mouth and whispered, real slow, "Cindy Ruggles thinks he's . . . a spy."

Suddenly my think-box kicked in. "A spy? Yeah! Maybe he's really a midget?"

The girls stopped, looked at me like I was from Jupiter, then busted up laughing.

"You're pretty funny, Bird," said Susan.

"Want to sit with us at lunch tomorrow?" Minnie asked.

Of course they didn't realize I was being serious, but I didn't say anything. It felt kind of good to be laughed *with* instead of laughed *at*, so I figured, Why blow it, now that I was in the gang for once.

"Okay, see ya tomorrow." I waved goodbye before splitting off toward the meadow. The others headed the opposite way, toward their houses on one of the newer tree-lined streets in town. No one else walked home in my direction.

* * *

In the woods, I kicked through the grass and broken twigs, studying my P-40 manual. I knew it was filled with stuff most kids thought was boring, like rpm's and oil-pressure gauges and altimeter readings and emergency procedures and stuff. But I loved reading it. For some reason it made me feel closer to Dad and helped me not to miss him so much. I had just about got it memorized, all except the last chapter, on landing.

I got to a part of the woods where the thick trees blocked most of the daylight, making it hard to read. Then, amid all the normal chirping of birds and rustling of branches in the wind, I got a sudden chill. It was a strange feeling, like when Farley stuck that Kick Me sign on my back and I could feel everyone watching me.

I shrugged it off and kept walking, stopping only when I noticed my darn shoe was untied again. But as I bent down to tie it, a twig snapped—behind me.

See, the thing was, my dad told me animals in the woods don't break twigs. They have a natural sense of how to step over twigs so they can move quietly.

"Hello?" I called out, foolishly. I mean, everyone knows that when you're scared, no one ever answers you back.

The woods were suddenly really quiet. I looked around. I saw nothing but long shadows where the light broke through the trees. Then a cloud blocked the sun, making it even darker.

I started walking again and immediately heard rustling,

sort of like footsteps. I stopped again, and when I did, so did the footsteps.

"Who's there?"

I could hear my voice crack and echo through the trees before it died.

"Farley Peck! You're gonna be sorry."

Silence.

Too much silence. I mean, Farley Peck could never be that silent in a million years.

My eyes shot side to side. I started again, this time at a fast walk.

But the footsteps moved faster, too.

I was getting really scared now and I decided to quicken my pace. What was it Dad said about not letting animals know you're afraid? But this wasn't even an animal (at least not a regular one), because it snapped the twig, right? So maybe acting afraid would scare it away?

Right. Who was I kidding? I was way too scared to *pretend* I wasn't scared. What if being scared was just my mind's way of telling me to get my butt the heck out of here?

So I ran.

Now the woods began to close in around me. Like long bony fingers, the branches clawed at me as I tried to escape. I kicked the moldy leaves out of my path, but a gnarled vine snared my foot and I stumbled and fell. I scrambled to scoop up my books, and once I was on my feet again, I was back into a full-out run.

But the footsteps fell faster and closer. They were almost

upon me. I could hear my heart pounding louder and louder—even louder than the first time Dad took me flying.

Suddenly a P-40 fighter plane that must have been on maneuvers roared its twelve cylinders overhead, somewhere above the trees. I ran blindly, gasping for breath, not looking back, not looking ahead, not until I ran smack into—

A man.

CHAPTER

"Aaaaahh!" I screamed with all my heart, but the scream was drowned out by the passing plane. Suddenly the tall man in uniform grabbed hold of me.

"It's okay," he said.

Relieved, I struggled to catch my breath. "Hi, Deputy. It was chasing me."

Deputy Steyer scanned the area. "What was?"

"A werewolf, I think."

He snickered. "Come on, Bird. I'll take you home."

Deputy Steyer had been in charge of law and order in Geneseo since Sheriff Gascon enlisted in the Marines. The deputy had moved to our town about six years ago, from Pennsylvania or New York, I think. He'd known me since kindergarten, when Mrs. Simmons called the cops to get me off the school roof.

He helped with my books and the P-40 manual slipped to the ground. The deputy picked it up. He read the cover. "What are you doing with this, Bird?"

"Memorizing it. I'm gonna fly one."

He looked around suspiciously, then drew me near and whispered, "Bird, if something like this got into the wrong hands . . ."

"You mean . . . the enemy?"

He nodded. "I'm going to have to keep it."

"But I'm almost done. I just need to memorize the section on landing."

"I'm sorry. But you know what they say—"

"Loose lips sink ships?"

He nodded again, then reached for the book.

"But . . . it was from my dad," I pleaded.

"I'm sorry." He took it from my hands.

It really stunk to have to hand it over. Why is it always like that? The thing you love the most turns out to be the one thing that can hurt you the worst. Like too many gumdrops. Or Amelia Earhart wanting to fly around the world. Like me, she had loved flying more than anything. She had to try to circle the globe. So she took off and was never seen again.

But I guess I understood. I mean, anything I could do to keep Dad safe was a good enough reason for me, right?

At the edge of the woods, the land sloped to the shore of the bay. I could see Father Krauss holding his fishing rod and talking with a white-haired fisherman, Mr. Ramponi.

"I tell you, Carlo, it was no fish," Father Krauss was saying. "It nearly pulled my boat under."

Deputy Steyer and I started down the slope. "Hi, Father," the deputy said. "Afternoon, Mr. Ramponi."

Father Krauss was nothing like our old priest. When you saw him without his collar on, he looked more like a longshoreman—you know, big shoulders and a chest like a barrel. I once asked why he became a priest and he said it was so he could be a linebacker for Jesus.

"Bird said someone was chasing her in the woods," the deputy told them.

"Not someone. Some*thing*." I straightened him out.

"Is that you, Bird?" Father Krauss said. He was pretending he couldn't recognize me because I was in a dress. "Where's your pilot's cap?"

"Mom said I can't wear it to school anymore."

Mr. Ramponi examined the broken line on Father Krauss's reel. "Yep. Look like the Genny that tore my nets last month." Mr. Ramponi was only about half the size of Father Krauss, but you'd never have known it when you saw him single-handedly haul in his fishnets. He had forearms like Popeye's. Sometimes he was hard to understand, but I liked to hear him talk because, when he did, he would get all excited and use his whole body.

"Don't joke around, Carlo," Father Krauss scolded him. "You'll frighten the girl."

"The *Genny*?" asked Deputy Steyer.

"Where you come from, boy?" Mr. Ramponi said scornfully. "The city? Tell him, Bird."

"Can I?"

Father Krauss rolled his eyes, but Mr. Ramponi elbowed him and said to me, "Go on."

I acted it out for Deputy Steyer as I went. "Well, she's a giant, slithering serpent that lures greedy fishermen out of the bay in the dark of night. And then, when they least expect it, she swallows them whole! I've seen her."

"You've got quite an imagination, Bird," said Deputy Steyer.

Father Krauss just shook his head. "Well, whatever it was that snapped my line, it would've been a record for sure."

"If you say so, Father," said the deputy skeptically. "Come on, Bird. Your mother will be worried."

"I guess so." I waved goodbye to Father Krauss and Mr. Ramponi and then shuffled on my way with the deputy.

When we got to my house, Mom was in the kitchen boiling turnips and cooking beans. I walked in with Deputy Steyer and the first thing she noticed was my tattered homemade frock.

"My dress!" Mom screamed.

"I didn't do it on purpose," I told her.

"Get into the tub this instant," she ordered. "And no radio tonight. You'll eat dinner in your room."

I slumped toward the stairs.

"She said something was chasing her in the woods," the deputy said.

But Mom didn't buy it. "You know Bird. Wherever she goes, her imagination's not far behind."

"Of course," he said.

"Thanks for looking out for her, and for bringing her home," Mom said. "That was really thoughtful of you, Deputy."

He smiled like he was kind of embarrassed. "Just keeping things safe on the home front."

Two hours later I was still stuck in my room with nothing but a plate of cold turnips on the nightstand, so I decided to write a letter.

Dear Dad,

I miss you more than ever. Mom doesn't understand me like you do.

No one does.

I paused. My stomach tightened from hunger. I tried to force down some cold turnip, but it tasted like wet plaster. "Yuck." But then I started to wonder what Dad was eating for supper. I bet he would have given anything to be there dining on Mom's undercooked turnips for the tenth day in a row. I downed another slice of turnip, for Dad.

I could hear my mom downstairs, fighting with the sewing machine, trying to save my dress. I always thought she hated sewing, but ever since the war started it was like she was trying to prove she was Betsy Ross or something. Margaret said Mom was just trying to keep her mind off Dad.

Alvin was in the front room listening to my favorite radio program, *The Green Hornet*. It was just loud enough that I could recognize the theme music. I thought I heard the Green Hornet shoot his gas gun but I couldn't tell whether Kato and the Black Beauty arrived in time to save Casey from the Creeper.

I could tell Margaret must have been winding rag curlers in her hair because every few minutes I heard her yelp like a cocker spaniel.

Suddenly the doorbell rang and I jumped right out of my bed. You see, out where we lived our doorbell almost never rang, especially at night. After a moment I could hear Mom's slow, measured footsteps cross to the door. I ran to the top of the stairs and stuck my head through the banister to see. As Mom opened the door, I noticed that her hand was shaking.

On our doorstep were two Army Air Corps officers standing at attention, one behind the other. The older one in front took off his hat.

"Mrs. McGill?" he asked.

Mom took a deep breath. Like she was bracing herself for something bad, which made my hand clutch the banister.

"I'm Captain Winston; this is Lieutenant Peppel." The captain stepped aside.

Lieutenant Peppel stepped forward, head bowed. "Ma'am, I'm awful sorry."

Mom covered her mouth. "Oh God!"

"The lieutenant thought it was part of the exercise, Mrs. McGill," the captain explained.

"I had no idea your little sprout was gonna be out on that airfield this mornin'," said the young lieutenant.

With one big sigh of relief, Mom said, "Bird."

The captain seemed confused. "Bird? Ma'am?"

"Won't you come in?" Mom said.

In the living room the captain explained, "When we contacted the school, one of the teachers remembered your daughter coming in covered with flour."

Mom hollered upstairs, "Bird!"

I came the rest of the way downstairs and Mom introduced everybody. "Captain Winston and Lieutenant Peppel, these are my children, Alvin, Bird, and Margaret."

The lieutenant was kind of skinny, with a crooked grin and a fuzzy shadow on his lip that looked like he was trying to grow a mustache but really couldn't yet. He had pale blue eyes. They weren't as gentle or as blue as Dad's, but I could tell Margaret was already all goo-goo eyed over them.

She rolled out a girly *"Hello."*

"It's a pleasure to meet you, Miss McGill," the lieutenant said, and he kissed her hand. Yuck. I thought I was gonna throw up.

Margaret nearly swooned. "I just love the way you talk," she said. "Are you from Texas?"

"I'm from Sweetwater, outside Atlanta, miss."

"Atlanta?" Margaret looked so dazed you'd have thought he just said his name was Rhett Butler. Ever since she saw *Gone With the Wind*, she'd been wishing she was Scarlett O'Hara.

"Uh, that's in Georgia, Margaret," I explained to her.

"I know that, Bird," she said haughtily.

"Whatever you say . . . Curly." I pointed to her curler-covered head.

Margaret felt atop her head and shrieked with horror, "Mom!" She lifted her pajama top to cover her hair, and instead exposed her bra.

Without missing a beat, Alvin started to chant, "I see London, I see France, I see Margaret's underpants."

Red-faced, Margaret ducked and raced back up the stairs. But curlers or no curlers, the poor lieutenant seemed just as goo-goo eyed over her as she had over him. Maybe he needed glasses.

Then Mom said, "Bird, the lieutenant said he saw you on the airfield this morning."

"You were flying that Warhawk?" I asked him, finding it pretty hard to believe. I mean, *Mom* was taller than this kid.

"Yup. Sorry 'bout bombing ya, sprout," he apologized. "You okay?"

I looked him over and frankly, I wasn't too impressed. "You look barely old enough to drive."

He laughed and mussed my hair. "I'm nineteen, you little peach pit."

"Bird, I told you to stay away from the airfield," Mom said.

"Okay, Mom. I promise." I gave it a shot, but it wasn't one of my better performances. Behind my back, I made sure my fingers were crossed.

"Now, back to bed," Mom said.

I trudged up the stairs.

"Good night," the lieutenant called out to me.

Halfway up the stairs I paused to give him some advice I remembered from the manual: "Adjust your rudder trim and you'll get more airspeed diving." But the lieutenant and the captain just laughed as I scampered the rest of the way upstairs.

From my window I could hear Mom seeing them to the door. "You'll have to excuse Bird. She has this thing for airplanes."

"We're just glad she's okay." The captain sounded amused. Not amused like he really believed I knew anything about airplanes, but amused like the way people used to get when Dad told them I could throw a curveball.

While the captain talked with Mom, I saw the lieutenant

wander into the front yard. I could hear Margaret's big mouth gargling from the bathroom and my brain hatched an idea. I leaned halfway out the window and whispered out to Lieutenant Peppel, "*Pssst!* Hey, greenhorn."

"Hey," he answered.

"What would it take to get me a ride in your Warhawk?"

He shook his head. "You mean besides a commission in the Army Air Corps?"

"Listen. I've flown lots with my dad. And I know the P-40 backwards and forwards," I told him.

He looked up at me and smiled. "I bet you do. But it's still a pretty tall order, Peach-pit. You better leave the flying to us fighter pilots."

But he didn't realize I had a goo-goo-eyed ace up my sleeve. "What if I could arrange a rendezvous between you and a certain curly-haired Allied sympathizer?"

"Rendezvous?" Bingo! His eyes lit up like Judge Dickens's Christmas tree. "And you're sure she'd go out with me?"

I turned toward the bathroom and saw Margaret trying on Mom's lipstick. "Let's just say my intelligence sources promise little or no resistance."

I could see he was about to take the bait, when the captain called, "Lieutenant, let's go."

With time running out, I scrambled for something that would seal the deal. I quickly grabbed one of Margaret's bras, which happened to be nearby. I stuck it out the window and twirled it around my finger. "I can guarantee it."

Lieutenant Peppel's eyes were practically bugged out. "All right, Peach-pit. I'll be in touch."

"Roger Wilco." I gave him my best Army Air Corps salute and watched him drive away with the captain.

CHAPTER 7

The next day at school, I kept busy sketching in my notebook, while Mrs. Simmons slowly worked her way through the class, assigning report topics for each of us. My drawing was really cool. It showed me piloting a P-40 Warhawk and strafing the Genny in the bay with my wing-mounted machine guns. *D-d-d-d-d-t-t-t-t!* Luckily, no one had taken my topic yet—"The Curtiss P-40: Greatest Plane in Rhode Island"—so I was pretty jazzed. I imagined someday, when I was a world-famous fighter ace, I was gonna fly to a desert island and find Amelia Earhart. I didn't believe it when people said she was dead. I bet she was on an island, drinking coconut milk and lying in a hammock safe and sound.

Mrs. Simmons moved down the list to Minnie. "And your report topic, Miss Lashley?"

"President Roosevelt," Minnie announced loudly so everyone could hear.

"What's he got to do with Rhode Island?" Libby complained.

"My father said he's making a whistle-stop in Providence this July," Minnie answered.

"Excellent, Minnie. Susan? What about you?"

"Um. I don't know."

Uh-oh. Wrong answer. But before Susan could blink, Mrs. Simmons had her assigned. "How about the state flower, hmm?"

Susan groaned. I had learned the hard way you'd better be ready with your topic or else Mrs. Simmons would stick you with one of the boringest ones. I'm talking about the kind that would put even Mr. Van Dyke, the science teacher, to sleep (and he liked to make mold).

Finally it was my turn. I leapt to my feet. "I want to do it on—"

"Bird, sit down. Kenji is next," Mrs. Simmons said.

"Oh. I guess I didn't see him there." I slumped back down into my seat. *Come on, just pick your stupid topic so I can go.*

Kenji peeked out from behind some movie star magazine he had hidden inside his arithmetic book. He stood up and said, without an ounce of enthusiasm, "My uncle works at that factory outside of town. He said they make the engines for the plane John Wayne flies in his new movie, *The Flying Tigers*."

Mrs. Simmons corrected him, proud of our little town's important contribution to the war effort. "Oh. You mean the P-40 Warhawk."

"Yeah, whatever. Could I do a report on that?"

"What an original idea. That would be splendid. Okay, now you can go, Bird."

Splendid? It wasn't splendid. It was awful. So awful I was speechless. I glared at Kenji.

"I don't have all day," said Mrs. Simmons. "Shall I choose one for you?"

In a daze, all I could mumble out was "Huh?"

"How about the state marsh weed?" she said with a straight face.

My mouth dropped open but I was too outraged to speak.

"Marsh weed it is. And remember, everyone: footnotes."

The class groaned all together. As the bell rang and the students filed out, I was too shocked to even drag myself out for gym class.

By the time I did trudge outside, the boys were picking baseball teams, so I snuck over to watch. They were splitting off to head for the diamond when Mr. Phelps, the gym teacher, noticed that Kenji was left behind.

Mr. Phelps collared Farley and pointed at Kenji. "Hey. What about that kid?"

Raymond had to think quick. So he kicked Kenji in the shin.

"Ow!" Kenji yelped.

"He's got a bad leg," Raymond explained.

Then Red Phillips, an obnoxious kid with too many freckles, piped up. "And what do Japs know about baseball anyway?"

"Besides, he doesn't want to play," added Farley.

But as anyone could tell you, that argument didn't work with Mr. Phelps. Sports were his life. He wore sneakers and sweat socks all day, every day, even to church.

"Listen," he said. "In my class, everybody plays." He walked over, grabbed Kenji, and pushed him along to join them. "I've got to umpire for the girls. Any trouble, you just holler."

A half hour later, it was the bottom of the last inning, two outs, with Farley on the mound holding on to a one-run lead and looking for blood. He wound up, hurled his meanest curveball, and hit Frankie Mitchell hard in the back.

Raymond hollered from shortstop, "Atta boy, Farley."

"Atta boy?" their second baseman, Dickie Doolittle, shot back at Raymond. "That's a walk, you idiot."

"It's all right." Raymond shrugged, trying not to seem so dumb. "We still got 'em by a run."

Frankie hobbled to first. But as soon as Farley turned his back, Frankie took off for second. He was faking being hurt! By the time Farley noticed, Frankie was already safe at second with a stolen base.

All the players on Frankie's team jumped to their feet, rattling the dugout fence, cheering and clapping for Frankie's great steal. Everyone, that is, except Kenji, who sat alone at the end of the bench.

I decided this was as good a time as any to straighten him out. So I walked over and poked him hard in the back. "You stole it."

"Huh?" he answered, turning toward me.

"And you didn't even know it was called a P-40," I said with disgust.

"The airplane? So?" He turned away.

"So?" I poked him in the back some more. "It was my topic. Everybody knew it was my topic. And you stole it."

Sean Fitzgerald, their catcher, called out, "Come on, Farley. One more out."

Red called his next batter. Kenji. "Hey, Charlie Chan, you're up."

But Kenji just played dumb. So I elbowed him, hard. "Hey, they're calling you."

Red clapped his hands. "Come on, Nip. Chop-chop."

Kenji rose slowly from the bench and walked over to Red. "For your information, Charlie Chan is Chinese. My name is Kenji."

"That's not my fault. Now listen. Know what this is?" Red held a tattered hardball under Kenji's nose. Kenji said nothing. "Didn't think so. It's a baseball, see? Now the point of the game is for that guy"—Red pointed to Farley—"to hit you with it. Just ask Lumpy."

Lumpy looked up from the bench and nodded. He was a chunky kid with baseball welts on his face and arms. His specialty was getting beaned. Lumpy had drawn a walk every at-bat for the last two years. When he smiled, Kenji saw that he was minus quite a few teeth.

"After you, Tiny's up next," said Red.

Kenji spotted Tiny, a miniature Babe Ruth, fanning a Louisville Slugger in the on-deck circle.

"He'll knock you in," Red explained, "and we win. See? It's so simple, even you can understand it."

Kenji turned and marched to the plate. He picked up the bat and held it at an odd angle.

Farley wound up and called out, so everyone could hear, "This is for Pearl Harbor, guys," and whistled one right past Kenji's head, flattening him to the dirt. Kenji accidentally swung his bat in the process. Strike one.

"Like a turkey shoot," gloated Farley.

"Except this time it's a chicken," Raymond chimed in.

Figuring out Red's strategy, the catcher, Sean, said, "Stop fooling around, Farley. If he gets on, Tiny's up next."

Sean was right. Tiny hit at least a double every time he came up to bat. If Farley beaned Kenji and put him on base, odds were pretty good that Tiny would get a hit and win the game. Farley needed to get Kenji out to seal the victory.

Kenji climbed back to his feet. Dusted himself off. From the bench, Red and his teammates signaled Kenji to lean into the pitch. He just ignored them. Farley launched another pitch, straight for his head. Kenji sidestepped and swung again—strike two.

Sean returned the pitch. "Atta boy, Farley. One more."

By this time, most of the other kids in gym class were finished with their games and heading back toward the schoolhouse. A small crowd began to gather to watch Farley strike out the new Japanese kid.

Red marched angrily up to Kenji. "What's a matter? No speaka da English? You got to let it hit you if you want a walk."

Kenji shoved him aside. He dug his feet into the batter's box. Set his jaw. Tightened his steely focus on the ball. Then . . . complete silence as Kenji pointed his arm out to center field, just like Babe Ruth calling his shot.

Who did this kid think he was? He cocked the bat like it was some kind of medieval catapult. That was when the other kids in the crowd started to laugh.

But for some reason, I didn't.

Farley snickered. He pounded his fist into his mitt.

"Lights out, Hirohito." Farley wound up like a spring. And hurled one last blistering curveball with everything he had.

Crack!

It sounded like a thunderclap. But there wasn't a cloud in the sky. Only a white ball shooting like a rocket up to outer space.

GOODBYE, MR. SPAULDING! Kenji had creamed it harder than Farley or any kid I had ever seen—even seventh graders. That ball sailed like it had wings, over the helpless outfielders, landing at least twenty feet outside the fence.

Raymond called out to Farley, "Maybe you should've beaned him?"

"Shut up," snarled Farley.

I had to admit, I was pretty impressed. Maybe even a little jealous.

Kenji's teammates cheered him, but the funny thing was, he made no motion to run the bases.

Red patted him on the back. "You're all right for a Jap."

But Kenji turned away with the bat on his shoulder. There was a strange look in his eyes.

"Hey, you gotta run the bases." Red laughed nervously.

Kenji ignored him and began walking to the schoolhouse.

"Hey! What about the game?" Red shouted.

Kenji stopped, turned, and answered in a pretty good imitation of Clark Gable, "Frankly, freckle-head, I don't give a darn." Then he tossed the bat in the dirt—and just walked away.

Sean and Red began to argue over whether Kenji needed to round the bases for it to count. Farley just stood there, pounding his fist in his mitt, grinding his teeth, and getting red in the face.

I watched quietly and found myself wishing that I had been able to do that to Farley.

CHAPTER

On Saturdays I would usually go to the movies. In fact, every kid in Geneseo would go to the movies. But thanks to Kenji, this Saturday I had to go research "the official Rhode Island marsh weed." At the movie theater they would show newsreels before the features. The week before, the Fox Movietone News had a story on the German U-boat wolf packs in the Atlantic, and the amazing Doolittle Raid on Japan. I had been trying to remember all the names and places (in case Dad got sent there or wrote about them once he was shipped out), but it was hard because they all sounded so stupid and weird.

As I walked past the Bijou on Main Street, kids were lining up for *Only Angels Have Wings*, that week's Saturday matinee feature, starring Cary Grant. Just my luck, a picture about pilots on the one day I couldn't go. I bet Dad would have really liked that one, too. I remember one time, when I was in second grade, Dad snuck me out on a school night to see this silent movie about World War One pilots called *Wings*. To tell the truth, except for the flying scenes, it was kind of boring, but I pretended to love it as much as Dad did. I think that made him enjoy it even more. Afterwards he caught heck from Mom for sneaking me out, but he said it was worth it. I wished I could have snuck Dad out of the Army Air Corps to see this one with me. This time I wouldn't have had to pretend to like it, because just having Dad sitting next to me would have made it the best movie I ever saw.

I passed by Minnie, Susan, and Libby. They said "Hi," made a few wisecracks about my overalls, and tried to get me to stay, but when I told them I couldn't, they went right back to giggling about how "dreamy" Cary Grant looked on the movie poster.

I spotted Kenji hopping off the back of his uncle's bicycle, which was weighted down with all kinds of junky-looking fishing gear.

"Are you sure you'll be okay?" his uncle asked.

"I'll be fine, Uncle," Kenji said.

I noticed Farley and Raymond smoking a cigarette in the alley, by the trash can. The way they were eyeballing

Kenji, I didn't think he was gonna be *fine*. But I didn't tell him that. I didn't say anything. I had marsh weeds to pick.

Along the shore of the bay, I stomped through the cattails in my dad's oversized trout-fishing hip boots, buried halfway to my waist in slimy green gunk. I tried to shoo away the mosquitoes buzzing around my head, but they came right back.

"How about the official Geneseo marsh weed?" I whined aloud to myself in my best imitation of Mrs. Simmons. I reached down and grabbed a bunch of weeds and yanked them out by the roots. Then something in the mud grabbed my attention. Clearing the weeds some more, I found it. A strange coil of copper wire. But before I could think about what it was—

"Ahoy, there!"

I jumped about a foot and landed with my butt in the mud. I peered back through the weeds and saw a rowboat, a little ways offshore. It was Father Krauss, along with Mr. Fujita, Kenji's uncle, back from fishing. They ran the boat aground and hopped out.

I stood up and brushed myself off. "Any sign of the Genny?" I called out.

Father Krauss snickered. "No. Not much of anything biting, I'm afraid."

Kenji's uncle quietly thanked Father Krauss and gathered his things to leave.

"No? What about tomorrow, Tomo?" Father Krauss asked.

"No. I cannot," Mr. Fujita said. "But thank you." He nodded to me and hurried into the woods on foot.

Father Krauss finished pulling the boat ashore.

"I guess he doesn't like me much, huh?" I said.

"It's not you, it's me," Father Krauss explained. "Mr. Fujita thinks he and I shouldn't fish together so much anymore. He thinks people might not like it if I'm friends with someone who's Japanese. I told him he's being foolish, but he's concerned for my well-being." Then Father Krauss noticed my hands and butt covered in muck. "What on earth have you been up to, Bird?"

"Um, looking for marsh weeds."

"Hope your luck's better than mine." He held up just one sickly-looking fish on his string and shook his head woefully. "Saints alive. Sister Marilyn's gonna have my head."

I laughed to think that Father Krauss might be as terrified of Sister Marilyn as all of us kids were. She was short, but she was about as wide as she was tall, like she'd been inflated with a tire pump. She had the uncanny ability to hear a swear word whispered from the farthest corner of the room during Sunday school, and other than Mrs. Storms, the town librarian, Sister Marilyn was the most vicious ear-pincher I ever knew. To top that off, you could never make faces when her back was turned, because she really did seem to have eyes in the back of her head.

"She's crankier than usual because of all the turnips in

the victory garden. With all the food rationing, we've had to eat them every night for a month." He put the back of his hand to the side of his mouth and whispered, grinning, "They give her *gas*." He patted me on the head and went on his way.

Once he was gone, I dropped my weeds and plopped down in his rowboat. My arms were pretty sore from pulling weeds and swatting mosquitoes all afternoon, so I figured I would just lie back and rest for a minute or two. I squinted at the puffy clouds overhead and closed my eyes, wondering where Dad was, and whether he was missing me as much as I was him.

"Ow!" I felt a mosquito bite my cheek, but when I swatted it, it stung my face like a bullwhip. *Yeow!* Sunburn. Unlike Margaret, who got tan every summer, I was pale and freckled and quickly burned. The whole side of my head felt like I could have boiled an egg on it. I peeled my eyes open and took a minute to adjust to how dark it had gotten. I realized I must have slept all afternoon. It had to be after eight, 'cause I could already hear the twilight katydids chirping.

And I could hear something else. Whistling.

It was coming from two people. The whistling was off-key, but I could sort of make out the tune. It was a tone-deaf version of "Don't Sit Under the Apple Tree," the Andrews Sisters' latest hit.

I stood up in the boat and scanned the woods, but I didn't see anyone,

Then I saw something move. Some branches. About forty yards away. I squinted my eyes and looked harder. It was Kenji, stepping out of the woods and walking toward me. But he wasn't whistling.

Farley and Raymond were. They came out of the woods about twenty yards behind him. I ducked down and watched through the weeds. Kenji didn't bother to turn around, just picked up his pace.

The whistling got faster, and so did Farley's and Raymond's footsteps. Suddenly Kenji broke into a full run.

When I looked back an instant later, Raymond and Farley had disappeared.

"Ha!" Kenji spun around and struck a mock karate pose. But no one was there.

A lonely owl hooted in the darkness and I tried to keep from snickering. I could see Kenji relax with relief just as—

A spotlighted ghost face appeared on the branches of the tree above him, laughing. It was Raymond with a flashlight under his chin. He hollered, "Sayonara, sucker!"

Suddenly Farley leapt out and grabbed Kenji from behind. "It's time Mr. B-b-baseball saw a real Yankee slider. Show him, Raymond." Farley held Kenji with his arms tight around him.

Raymond worked up a juicy hocker, which wasn't hard 'cause he was always sneaking his dad's chewing tobacco. Then he spit and let it fly at Kenji.

But at the last second, Kenji spun around perfectly so

that it was Farley who wound up blinded with an eyeful of tobacco juice.

"Ahhh!" Farley screamed.

Kenji broke free and took off, heading right for me. Raymond jumped down and fussed to clean up Farley. "I'm sorry, Farley."

Farley brushed him off. "Leave me alone! Just get him!"

Kenji ran hard, panicked. I knew exactly how he felt. I'd been there a hundred times with Farley hot on my heels. But the stink of marsh weeds was still fresh on my hands, reminding me who got me stuck with this lame report topic. "Serves him right," I said to myself.

The bullies were gaining, though, and I could see that Kenji was getting tired.

"You're gonna eat mud!" Farley snarled.

Finally my conscience kicked in. Not even Kenji deserved that. I tossed my weed collection into the boat and rocked the boat free.

"Hey! Over here," I yelled.

Kenji spotted me, but seemed suspicious.

"Stay out of this, Birdbrain!" Farley hollered when he saw me. He and Raymond speeded up as I started to cast off.

"Hurry!" I told Kenji. "Come on."

It was clear he had no choice but to trust me. He splashed through the water and flopped into the rowboat.

Farley and Raymond, neither one a good swimmer, sloshed into the water after us.

I quickly shoved the other oar into Kenji's hand. "Row, stupid!"

He did, but not very well. We rowed furiously, but our strokes were fighting each other, causing the boat to zigzag.

Suddenly Farley popped his head out of the water and grabbed hold of my oar. "Got you, Jap lover!" His grimy hands were a lot stronger than mine and it took all my weight to keep him from tipping the boat over.

But Kenji thought fast and swatted his oar, splashing water right up Farley's nose.

It worked! Farley started coughing out seawater and let go of my paddle.

After a few more sloppy strokes, Kenji and I found a one-two rhythm and we started to pull away. Farley and Raymond chased us as far as the sandbar cutoff, but once they went underwater and realized they couldn't touch bottom, they decided to retreat. Looking like two drenched rats, the bullies barked and bellyached from the shore.

"Chicken!" taunted Raymond.

"Traitor!" screamed Farley. "You'll pay for this, Bird."

As we pulled away, Farley and Raymond shrank in the distance. Feeling safe, I stopped rowing and let us drift into the bay.

"One thing about Farley, he swims about as good as an anchor," I joked.

Kenji was silent, catching his breath.

"Don't say thanks or anything," I snapped.

"Thanks," he said.

"It's the least I could do after you stole my report topic," I told him.

"I didn't steal it," he said. "Anyway, if you want it so bad, take it."

"What? You mean it?"

"It's just a stupid airplane," he said.

"Airplanes aren't stupid," I told him. "Especially Warhawks." Just what kind of weirdo was this kid? "Don't you know they had a ten-to-one kill ratio in China against the Japs?" Then I shut myself up. What was I saying? He *was* a Jap. "I meant, you know . . . the Jap-a-nese."

"I know what you meant," he said.

Great. Now it was gonna be a long uncomfortable silence and I'd probably say something stupid, like—

"My little brother still pees in this water when he goes swimming." *Oh my God!* I thought. *Did I really just say that?*

Kenji looked at me like I was a polka-dotted sea slug.

I couldn't help it. When things got quiet and uncomfortable, I'd sometimes say stupid stuff. Like once, we were all sitting around the Christmas dinner table waiting for Grandma to say grace—and she passed gas. I mean a really big one. But everyone pretended like she didn't and just held their breath while she kept on praying. Uncle Rupert was practically turning blue. Finally I couldn't take the silence and blurted out, "I didn't know you knew how to fart,

Grandma." I had to eat dinner in Grandma's cellar for that one, but Dad told me later that I probably saved Uncle Rupert from having an asthma attack.

"I just meant, you know, I wouldn't gulp down any of this water if you ever go swimming in the bay here," I explained.

"Sure," Kenji said. He reached into his jacket and carefully pulled out a soggy yellow Milk Duds box. It was empty. He pulled another one out of his shirt pocket. Nothing. Then he found a third one in his back pants pocket. He dug his fingers in deep and pulled out the sorriest-looking, most waterlogged chocolate-covered caramel I'd ever seen. He was about to pop it in his mouth when he felt me staring, and stopped.

"Milk Dud?" he said, offering it to me first.

"Uh, no thanks."

Kenji shrugged "okay" and started chomping away. His foot happened to bump the fishing rod in the boat, so he leaned over and picked it up, kind of gently.

"This your rod?"

"Nope. It's Father Krauss's."

"Oh."

He examined the assortment of fancy lures and treble hooks dangling on the lead.

I pointed to the silver lure with tiny mirrors on both sides. "That's his favorite lure."

"It's a pretty fancy setup," Kenji said.

"You fish?" I asked.

"My father used to. He's gone now."

"You mean . . . dead?" I said, surprised. I guess I hadn't really thought about how this kid ended up living with his uncle here in Geneseo.

"More or less," he said.

More or less? That didn't make sense. "How can someone be more dead, or less dead? You either are or you aren't, right?" I said. "What do you mean?"

"I mean, it's none of your business."

So I shut up. I'd found that was the best thing to do when someone said "It's none of your business." There were some things (like why Minnie's big sister Emily had to go live with her aunt after her belly started to get fat) that they'd never tell an eleven-year-old girl no matter how many questions she asked. I was trying to figure Kenji out, but it was almost like he was joking about his dad being dead. Or maybe he didn't care?

Kenji grabbed the rod and tossed the line into the water. "So, what do you catch around here?"

"Lately, nothing, because of the Genny," I said, matter-of-factly.

"What's the Genny?"

"Do you scare easy?" I asked.

"What do you think?" he scoffed. "I saw *Frankenstein* three times in a row, and I only shut my eyes once."

"Okay, you asked for it."

I had him just where I wanted him. So I began to relate the legend of the Genny.

"Well, many years ago, there was this strange and beautiful fisherwoman named Genny, who lived in those woods over there by the bay."

I let my voice trail off, and even to me, the distant woods immediately seemed more mysterious.

"She lived alone and sang strange songs at night, but she was the best fisher in the village, man or woman. Because of that, some people claimed she was a witch. They said she was very selfish and never threw any fish back, no matter how small. One year, after an especially long and cold winter, the fishing was very bad. Everyone's nets went empty all spring and summer. Only Genny seemed to be able to catch anything. All the other fishers grew jealous and angry. So one night, when she was sleeping on her boat, they wrapped her in her blanket, like a snake, and tossed her squirming and screaming into the icy black waters of the bay."

I splashed the water just a little to give him the full effect. Then I made sure to stop and wait for the water to calm and grow silent again.

"So . . . what happened?" he asked, his eyes big as golf balls.

I smiled. Now he was hooked.

"Well, after that," I went on, "there seemed to be plenty of fish for everyone. Tuna, mackerel, you name it. The nets always came up full, year after year. Soon the fishermen forgot all about Genny. Until one night. It was fifty years, to the very night, from the time she was drowned. It was a night kind of like this one. With a full moon. In fact, I think it was the very same night as tonight."

"Get out of here," Kenji said, squirming a little in his seat. He took a big gulp of air. "Really?"

"That night, all the fishermen were on their boats. It was the last day of their fishing trip. The water was very still, kind of like it is now."

I started to rise and rock the boat, just a little.

"When suddenly . . . a giant black serpent with huge fangs and the face of a woman burst to the surface! Then, one by one, the Genny devoured all of the fishermen who had killed her!"

Kenji's face was a quivering, ghostly pale sheet. He swallowed hard, then pulled himself together.

"Aw . . . that's a bunch of hooey."

"Hooey? You better not let the Genny hear you say that," I said.

"Oh, come on. It's just a story."

I look at him, deadly serious. "I've seen her."

"Oh, yeah? Where?"

I glanced at the mouth of the inlet and checked my bearings.

"It wasn't far from . . . right here."

At that moment, a violent tug on Kenji's fishing line yanked him out of his seat.

"Hey, how'd you do that?" he asked.

"I didn't do anything," I answered. Then I came to the horrific realization. "It's the Genny!"

I flashed Kenji the international thumbs-down sign as he struggled to keep from being pulled over the side of the boat.

"What the heck is that supposed to mean?"

"It's the pilot's signal to bail out," I told him.

He gripped Father Krauss's rod and reeled the line in furiously. "Are you gonna help or what?" he screamed.

That snapped me into action, and the two of us fought the line like we'd hooked Moby Dick. Whatever it was on the other end, it was a lot bigger and stronger than the two of us. I looked over the side and realized it was pulling us and Father Krauss's boat out of the bay.

"Reel her in slow!" I yelled. "She won't hurt us if she sees we're just kids."

"You're crazy!" Kenji yelled back. "Just cut the line!"

"You got money for a new set of lures?"

He shrugged and held on.

But just as quickly as it had stretched taut, the line suddenly went slack, and the boat drifted to a stop. Kenji's eyes bulged.

"It's going under us!"

"Pick up the slack," I said.

Kenji started reeling and reeling, but there was no tension on the line.

"Faster!" I ordered, panicked.

Finally the end of the fishing line appeared. The lures were all gone.

"The line's been cut," I said.

Kenji took a big breath and straightened himself, trying to hide the fact that his heart was most likely ready to pound out of his chest. "Probably just a lost seal or something," he fake-chuckled to himself.

"Right," I said. "Or a shark."

Then Kenji's foot bumped against something in the boat.

"Ahhh!" he screamed.

I peeked out between my fingers. But it was just an orange life jacket under his seat.

He tried to act tough, bending down to pick up the jacket. "Here. You better put this on."

"I'm no sissy," I told him. "Why don't you put it on?"

Kenji dropped the jacket. "You think I bought that silly story about the Genny? Come on."

"You were scared," I told him.

"Was not."

"Was so."

"I was not!" he hollered, stomping his foot on the life jacket.

"All right. Take it easy," I said, flapping my hands for him to calm down. We both suddenly realized how still and eerily silent the bay had become.

"You know, I ought to be getting home," Kenji said.

"Okay." I reached for the oars. "But admit it, you were a little bit scared."

He opened his mouth to protest, but before anything

came out, all of a sudden, it was like there was an earthquake on the water. The boat rocked and rose up, as if we were being lifted by a giant.

"What's happening?" Kenji cried.

KRRRRR, went a scrape like metal against the hull as something large and black slithered right beneath us.

"It's the Genny!" I cried out.

CRASHHH! In an instant we were a pair of Daisy dolls tossed into the sea. It felt like we were being caught in the whirlpool wake of a giant whale as the swirling force of the diving beast sucked me under. The last thing I heard before the water swallowed me up was Kenji screaming out, "Bird!"

CHAPTER

Underneath, there was nothing but silence. The water was black as tar. I felt myself rolling over and over in the rush of seawater. The worst part was, I had no sense of which way was up. My lungs began to ache, starving for oxygen. I was frantically paddling in the water, but for all I knew, I might have been heading for the bottom.

Then something brushed against my hand. I tried to pull away, but it grabbed on to me. It was Kenji's hand. Our hands locked and I felt myself being dragged through the water. After what seemed like an eternity, we reached the surface and I gasped for air.

Kenji helped me latch on to the floating life jacket—just in time to see a thin black neck rising out of the water only twenty feet away. The monster's back broke the surface momentarily.

"Look!" I screamed. Then my body stiffened as I realized that it wasn't the black neck of the Genny, but something even more incredible. It was the periscope of a black minisubmarine!

The submarine gently dove beneath Father Krauss's capsized rowboat like an immense water snake. And then it disappeared.

Kenji and I shivered and stared as the submarine's telltale propeller wake headed out the inlet toward the Atlantic Ocean. Too scared to speak, we used our last bits of energy to hold on to the life jacket, kicking and paddling for the Geneseo shore.

Once we reached the shore, we dragged our waterlogged bodies from the bay and collapsed in the smelly marsh weeds.

"I told you it wasn't the Genny," Kenji spit out between gasps of air.

"You mean you saw it, too?"

"Saw it?" he said. "It was only about ten inches away from us."

"I just wanted to be sure." I shrugged. "Sometimes I'm the only one who sees stuff."

"Well, not anymore. But what's a submarine doing here?" Kenji asked.

I thought it over, and there was only one explanation. "Spying," I answered.

"What?"

"We've got to tell the deputy."

Kenji shook his head. "He'll never believe us."

"Sure he will. You'll see."

As he started to stand up, Kenji suddenly grabbed his stomach, doubled over, and groaned.

"What's wrong? Are you hurt?" I asked.

"Naw. Too many Milk Duds."

"Come on," I said, climbing to my feet. "I'll get you some bicarbonate at my house."

We tried to slip in the back door, only to find that Deputy Steyer was already waiting with Mom, Margaret, and Alvin.

"Mom!" I ran to her.

"Thank goodness," said the deputy.

Mom kissed the crucifix around her neck. "Bird McGill, you had us worried sick."

Before I could stop myself, I blurted out, "You won't believe what we saw!"

"I'm sure we won't," said Margaret.

"At first, when it knocked our boat over, we thought it was the Genny," I blabbered excitedly. "But then Kenji and I saw it. A submarine!"

"What?" Deputy Steyer seemed genuinely concerned.

I gave Kenji an I-told-you-so look.

But Mom wasn't buying it. "That's the last straw, young lady. To your room."

"But Mom—"

"Get!"

I clutched the deputy's sleeve. "Deputy Steyer, you've got to believe us."

"Bird!" Mom hollered. Then she turned to the deputy to explain. "She makes up these stories because she misses her father."

"I understand," the deputy said.

Kenji shook his head, and now it was his turn to give *me* the I-told-you-so look.

"I think I'd better take your little friend home," said the deputy.

Little friend? What made him think Kenji was my friend?

"Kenji?" I said. Kenji looked at me kind of funny. "Go on. Tell him."

But Kenji just stood there, silent as one of those monks who take a vow of silence for God. The deputy tugged Kenji's wet shirtsleeve toward the door.

"That's the first time you've called me by my name," Kenji said to me before he was led out the door.

Later on, after Margaret and I had gone to bed, I got up and opened the window to search the night sky. Even the full moon couldn't brighten how dark the world looked to me right then. The night air creeping in chilled Margaret, and she rolled over, half asleep.

"For gosh sakes, Bird. Close the stupid window."

I closed it and climbed back into my bed.

Kenji. Ken-ji. Kenj-i? *Kenji.* I guess it wasn't such a weird name after you said it enough. I mean, if you thought about it, Bird might have seemed like a pretty silly name to some people. From my nightstand, I took a framed photo of me and Dad standing next to Mr. Watson's airplane. *Friend.* That was kind of a funny word, too. What was the *i* doing in there? But like Dad used to say, some things don't make sense, you just accept them the way they are. I held the picture close, shut my eyes, and tried to get some sleep.

"Didn't you hear what I said? It was a submarine!" I told them.

Minnie and Libby were fussing with their hair in the bathroom mirror. I fidgeted nervously as Susan considered what to do with my Amelia Earhart hairdo.

"It was right here," I insisted. "In Geneseo Bay." But they just laughed, ignoring me.

"It's too short for ribbons or barrettes." Susan was running out of ideas. "How do you usually wear it?"

"Under my hat," I said, giving up.

"Did you guys start your reports yet?" Minnie said.

"No," snapped Libby. She knew Minnie was only asking so she could brag.

"Well, I'm done with mine on President Roosevelt," said

Minnie. "My dad let me use some of his district attorney's stationery to write it."

"Yeah, well, my dad said Roosevelt's a Communist," Libby retorted.

"He is not," I protested loudly. Then I asked, "What's a Communist?"

The other girls looked at each other, thinking.

"Uh, you know," said Libby, "like a pianist. Only with communes."

"Oh," I said, still confused.

All at once we were interrupted by a ruckus outside in the hall. There was a loud slam, and then someone came flying through the girls' bathroom door. A boy.

"Eeeek!" Susan screamed.

I turned to see that it was Kenji—with his pants yanked to his ankles—suffering more of the same humiliating Farley Peck stuff that used to be reserved for me.

"Get out of here, you Peeping Tom!" Minnie demanded.

"Sorry," Kenji said. He struggled with his pants and tried the door—which, of course, was being held shut by Farley and Raymond.

"Now!" Minnie ordered. "Or we'll get Mrs. Simmons and you'll really be in trouble."

Kenji yanked the door with all his might. Only by this time, Farley and Raymond had let go and it cracked him pretty good in the face. Farley, Raymond, and everybody else started laughing—everybody, that is, except me. Kenji gathered up what was left of his dignity and bolted away. I followed the girls as they tumbled out into the hallway.

"What's so funny?" I protested over their laughter.

"You have to ask?" Libby snapped.

"Say, whose side are you on, anyway?" Minnie added.

Farley flashed his crooked yellow-toothed grin and poked his grimy finger in my chest. "Yeah, traitor. Whose side?"

I yanked Susan's stupid barrettes out of my hair and tossed them right in Minnie's face. "Not yours," I told them.

I caught up with Kenji outside, in the schoolyard. He was slumped down behind a tree.

"Hey."

He didn't answer. Just turned away and finished buckling his belt.

"Why don't you tell Principal Hartwig?" I said, trying to offer some sort of solution.

"Would it make any difference?"

I thought about it. Then I shook my head. "Naw."

He rose to his feet and started walking away.

"Wait a minute," I said.

"What?"

"How come you didn't back me up and tell the deputy about the sub?" I asked.

"If that flatfoot didn't buy it from a smart egg like you, why would he believe me?" he said.

"Smart? You think I'm smart?"

"Sure. You know all that stuff about airplanes, don't you?"

I felt funny inside. No one except Dad ever made me feel like it was a good thing to know stuff about airplanes.

"Face it, nobody would ever believe the two of us," he said.

He said *us*.

For some reason, I liked the sound of that. It meant we were kind of the same. Maybe if you were weird like me, it was best to be friends with someone else who was kind of weird, too. Or maybe it just meant I wasn't so weird after all.

"Say, what if we could prove it?" I said. "About the spies, I mean."

"Spies? What makes you think it was spies? How do you know it wasn't an American sub?"

"Because it had a three-blade propeller, remember?" I told him matter-of-factly. "Our subs have four blades."

He looked at me like I was nuts. "How do you know this stuff?"

I hung my head. Maybe we weren't the same. "I'm just weird, I guess."

"Naw. You're not." He nudged me with his shoulder. "No more than anyone else, anyway."

"Yeah?"

"Yeah."

"You know what? You're okay, Kenji," I told him.

"You mean, for a *Jap*?"

"No." I nudged him back. "I mean, for a boy."

This made both of us crack a smile.

"Friends?" I asked.

Kenji nodded. "Friends," he said. Then his eyes lit up. "You know, if we *could* prove there were spies in the bay, we'd be heroes."

"You think? Heroes?"

"Sure. I bet they'd give us anything we wanted." His eyes seemed to inflate with the possibilities.

I thought for a split second about the one thing I wanted most in the whole world right then. It was easy. "Maybe they'd send my dad home?"

"I'm sure they would," he said.

"All right. Let's do it," I told him. "Let's go catch us a spy submarine." I stuck out my hand and we spit-shook on it.

"It was a coil of copper radio wire or something, right here, I swear," I told Kenji. We had traveled most of the way along the south bay shore with no luck. I got the sense he was starting to doubt me. "One of these days I'm gonna take a picture, and then people will have to believe me."

"I believe you," he said.

"Really?"

He got a mischievous look on his face, like after he hit the home run against Farley. "You know, I've got a camera."

"That's great. Let's set it up."

But then Kenji shook his head. "What am I thinking? That sub's not gonna show up in the daytime. Too easy to spot."

"But it might at night," I pointed out.

"Sure. But the only way to get a picture at night is with a bright flash, like lightning or something."

"Wait." I stopped us in our tracks. "There." In the mud about three yards ahead of us there was a trail of man-sized footprints leading into the woods. I didn't know who or what had made them, but there was nothing back there but old tree forts. We nodded to each other, then followed them.

We were marching through the woods tracking the footprints when Kenji kicked something.

I knelt down and found it. "I guess our spy got hungry."

It was an empty baked beans can, raggedly cut open with a knife. I didn't know whether to feel relieved that whoever we were tracking was human and liked beans, or scared 'cause he had a knife and we didn't.

Then we heard rustling in the woods and I quickly dragged Kenji by the shirt into the weeds, where we lay flat. We peeked through the weeds and saw someone stooped low, carrying a knapsack. I couldn't make out his face, but I would have recognized those muddy, patched-together overalls anywhere.

"It's Farley," I whispered.

"Farley? What's he doing?"

"*Shhh.*" I shook my head. We waited a few seconds for Farley to pass by, and decided to follow him.

A short ways into the woods, Farley stopped below an

old tree house, now overgrown with oak leaves. It was the one Jack Smithers and Toby Kucharski had built five years before. But I knew they hadn't used it in a while and wouldn't be using it anytime soon. They were both in the Army now. We watched Farley climb up, carrying the knapsack. But he wasn't alone. The wood-plank door opened and he was greeted by a skinny, bearded man, who emerged slowly from inside the tree house. Farley handed his black-handled hunting knife to the man.

Kenji and I hid ourselves behind a tree.

"Farley? A spy?" Kenji whispered.

I shook my head. "I don't think so. That's his father."

Kenji took another look. Mr. Peck kept his head bowed, like he was ashamed to look Farley in the eye while he stuffed his mouth with some bread.

"What's he doing up in a tree?" Kenji asked.

"I don't know. I heard he got called by the draft board last month, and then disappeared."

"Whaddya know, the big bully's dad is a yellow-bellied draft dodger," Kenji whispered with a certain glee. "It figures."

Draft dodger. That made me think about my dad, probably far away on some ship at sea, and I was suddenly mad as heck. "It's not fair," I blurted out. "My dad had to go."

Thanks to my big mouth, Farley heard me. He scanned the woods . . . and spotted us. Farley scrambled down from the tree house, and Kenji and I took off.

"Go that way!" I told Kenji. We split up, going on

opposite sides of a big weeping willow tree, and of course Farley stuck with me.

I was pretty quick and all, but Farley was still a year older. He tackled me at the woods' edge. "Where do you think *you're* going, Jap lover?" He got hold of my collar and throttled me.

"To the police, draft dodger," I spit back at him.

He shrank back a little. "You d-d-do and I'll pound you."

Suddenly Kenji pounced on Farley's back. "You 'd-d-do' and we'll tell the cops you helped your dad escape."

"You rat fink." Farley swatted him off like a fly and then let me go. "I ought to pound you right now."

Kenji helped me up. "Come on, Bird."

"Wait! Listen. If you keep quiet, I won't take your lunch money for a month." Farley actually looked scared.

"You're nuts," Kenji told him. He grabbed me and we kept walking.

Farley ran and stopped in front of us. "Two months."

"Forget it. Your dad's a draft dodger," I told him, poking my finger in his chest.

"Shut up," Farley said. "It's not his fault. He just isn't a killer."

"My dad went, and he's not a killer," I said.

"Of course he is, Birdbrain. Killing is what soldiers do," Farley said.

That caught me off guard. I guess I had never really thought about what my father would have to do in the war.

"My d-d-dad's not hurting anybody," Farley went on.

"He's hurting everybody, stupid," Kenji informed him. "Especially you. You're ashamed of him."

The truth of what Kenji said hit Farley worse than if he had been socked in the gut. I mean, he almost looked like he was about to cry, for Pete's sake.

"Leave him alone, Kenji." I don't know why I said it. Then I told Farley, "We'll think about it."

"What?" said Kenji.

"In the meantime, Farley, you promise to leave us alone," I said. "And make sure everyone else does, too."

Farley thought it over.

"Promise," I said.

Then he nodded, even though I could tell he didn't want to. "All right."

"What the heck did you do that for?" Kenji demanded as we walked side by side. I hadn't been paying attention to how far we had walked, and now I noticed we were on the dingier side of town.

"I don't know. It was the first time I ever felt sorry for him," I said with a shrug.

"I don't. If my big brother had deserted, they'd have shot him," Kenji said.

"You have a brother?" I said, surprised.

Kenji bit his lip, like the truth had just slipped out. "Uh, yeah. His name's Kiyo. He joined the army the day after the war broke out."

"How come you never told me about him?"

"I don't know," Kenji said. "I haven't seen him in a year."

"I guess you must miss him."

"Yeah," Kenji said, turning away.

He stopped out front of a run-down building with a broken porch. I remembered it now. My mom said it used to be some kind of a saloon for ladies, until Minnie's grandma got it closed down. Now it was called Francine's Rooming House.

"You live here?" I asked.

"Yeah," Kenji said. "Why? What's wrong with it?"

"Nothing," I said, not really telling the truth. It wasn't exactly what I'd call a home, but I guess it was probably the only place in town where he and his uncle could stay. I mean, they were Japanese, after all.

"I guess I'll see ya." Kenji started to head in.

"Hey. What about the camera?" I said.

"Do you really want to see it?"

"Sure," I said.

He hesitated. "Okay, come on in." He led me around to the back door.

We walked down a long hall. A lot of the doors were open. It was dark and it smelled kind of funny, from all the weird food cooking in the different rooms. We went past the bathroom and several rooms, one with a Negro family, several with old people speaking like Mr. Ramponi, and then one with people speaking another language that I couldn't understand.

When we finally got to the set of rooms where Kenji lived

with his uncle, I was surprised because it was much nicer inside. It wasn't very big, but there were a lot of fancy decorations and stuff. Kenji set down his jacket over a small photo on the shelf and closed the door.

"I'll get the camera," he said, and he went into the bedroom. While he was gone I looked around. I couldn't resist going to the shelf to uncover the photo. It was of a Japanese man and woman, pretending to smile as they stood in front of a military-style hut in the desert. Next to it was a stack of letters. The envelopes were all cut open and stamped INSPECTED BY U.S. GOVERNMENT. The return address included a strange word: *Manzanar.* I put the letters back, covered the picture back up, and wandered around.

In the kitchen I saw a stack of cardboard cylinders next to some colored paper and a jar of black powder, like pepper.

"What are you making, dynamite?" I asked.

Kenji called out from the other room, "My uncle makes fireworks for the Fourth of July."

On the wall there was a cool movie poster for a sailor picture called *The Long Voyage Home.* Looking closer, I noticed that the poster was actually signed by John Wayne.

"Say, do you know John Wayne?" I asked.

I heard Kenji digging in a box in the other room. "Sort of. I mean, I met him once. He was filming a movie where my dad's boat was docked."

"So you're from California?"

He called out, "Um, yeah. San Pedro—I mean, Hollywood."

"My mom calls it 'the place where dreams come true,' "
I said.

"For some people, I guess." He walked in and handed me
a shiny new Graflex camera, the kind newspaper reporters
used. "Here it is."

I took a look through the viewfinder. "Wow. I saw one of
these in *Life* magazine."

"You like it?" he said.

"Who wouldn't?"

"It's got a high-speed shutter and universal focus, so all
your shots come out sharp." I got the feeling he was showing off a bit. "But even with a flashbulb at night it's probably still too dark to work," he said.

"Yeah, I guess I didn't think about that." I glanced at the
cardboard tubes on the table and it came to me. "Say, what
if you shot off some of your uncle's fireworks? You know,
like a giant flashbulb?"

"Hey. That might actually work."

I spotted something through the viewfinder, across the
room. "Is that your uncle's phonograph?"

"Nope. It's mine."

"No way. Your very own?" I didn't get it. If his family
could afford to give him all this stuff, what was he doing
living in this place?

"Sure. What do you want to hear? Some bebop or some
boogie-woogie?"

"I don't know. Anything," I told him.

He started fanning through a bookshelf of records.

"We hardly ever listen to records anymore since my dad left," I said. "Mom said our phonograph needs a new needle, but I think it's because the music makes her too sad."

Kenji held up an old record. He dusted off the cover and said "Yeah," like he knew exactly what I meant. The cover had a really goofy drawing of a man and woman riding a bicycle and looking like they were about to kiss. It made me think of those corny old love songs from when my dad and mom were young.

"You worry about your dad?" Kenji asked.

"All the time." Just thinking about him then made me worried. Gosh, if I didn't watch it I was gonna start bawling right in front of Kenji. I ducked my head away, just in case.

Kenji squeezed my shoulder softly. Kind of the way Dad would. "Hey," he said, "if he's anything like you, he'll be okay."

"Thanks."

Kenji went back to his records, pausing now and then to consider an especially jazzy-looking one. But something still didn't make sense to me. How would a kid like Kenji get all this stuff? Finally I figured it out.

"This stuff was your parents', wasn't it?"

"No." He stopped fanning through the records. Then, reluctantly: "Yeah."

It got real quiet all of a sudden. And seeing how me and

quiet don't exactly get along, I was just about to ask something stupid about his parents when Kenji quickly plucked out a record.

"You ever hear this one?" he asked.

He wound the crank on the phonograph and lowered the needle. A rousing jitterbug number blared out. Kenji started to dance a little, doing a few fancy steps, and I had to admit, he was pretty darn good.

"Want me to show you?" he asked.

"I don't know."

"Come on," he said. "It's easy. My mom taught me."

He grabbed my hand and started slow, stepping back and forth. Dipping down. Left. Right. Left. Right. At first it was strange to be holding hands and I kept stepping on his feet, but after a minute or two I started to get the rhythm of the music. Then Kenji worked up to spinning me and I ducked under his arm. We did it just like grown-ups in the movies! I was surprised at myself. It was kind of easy. We did it again. Boy! I was dancing. I wished my dumb sister Margaret could have seen this. *She* had to take lessons all summer just to learn to square dance. Before long we were twirling like Fred Astaire and Ginger Rogers. And for the first time, I saw Kenji break into a real smile.

"Now for the big finish," he said.

The music started to build. Kenji got ambitious and tried to pick me up by my waist. But his hand got caught in the bib of my overalls, and instead we slipped and collapsed all over each other like Laurel and Hardy. After a second, we looked at each other and burst out laughing—just as Uncle Tomo walked in, home from working at the factory.

"Kenji!" he said. Then he hollered something in Japanese.

Kenji hopped to attention and yanked up the record needle. "Nothing, Uncle."

"Oh, we have company," Uncle Tomo said, recognizing me. He bowed. "Hello, Miss McGill."

"Hello." I clumsily tried to bow back to him the same way he had to me.

Uncle Tomo asked Kenji, "Now you want to be Ginger Roger?"

"It's Fred Astaire, Uncle. Ginger's the girl," Kenji said, embarrassed.

Uncle Tomo winked at me knowingly. "What happened to wishing you were John Wayne?"

"Uncle!"

"All right, all right. Miss McGill, you stay for dinner?"

"Thank you, sir, but I should be getting home," I told him.

Kenji walked me out into the hall.

"Do you think you could sneak us some of your uncle's fireworks?" I asked.

He fidgeted. "I don't know. Maybe."

"You know, you've never told me what you want if this crazy scheme works and they make us heroes," I said.

"I don't know. I haven't thought about it."

"Haven't thought about it? How could you think about anything else? I can barely pay attention in school."

"Who can, with that blabbering Mrs. Simmons teaching?"

We shared a laugh at that one.

"Do you think you'd go back to Hollywood?" I asked.

"Maybe," he said. But he didn't seem so sure.

"What about your uncle? I mean, if you went back to California, who would you live with?"

"I haven't thought about it, okay?" Kenji dropped his head.

"Okay, okay," I said. I guess I was talking too much. "So we'll meet by the south shore, Friday night?"

He nodded.

"And bring the camera," I reminded him.

I was a little ways down the hall when he called after me. "Say, Bird?"

"Yeah?"

He hesitated, then asked, "What's your real name?"

"Why do you want to know?"

"I don't know," he said.

I shrugged. "It's stupid."

"Okay. Forget it," he said. "It's no big deal."

"It's just . . . Everybody laughs at it," I said.

"I wouldn't," he said.

"Yeah? Well, maybe someday I'll tell you."

CHAPTER 10

When I walked into our kitchen, Mom was cutting up turnips and carrots for dinner. I twirled past her, practicing one of the dance steps Kenji had been teaching me. She looked at me and I raced back to wipe my feet. "Sorry," I said.

"What, sweetheart?" she said.

Sweetheart? She had never called me that before. Then I spotted a torn-open envelope on the table—and it had a Georgia postmark.

"A letter from Dad?"

Mom nodded, beaming, and I grabbed it.

"Your father's getting leave in July," Mom said. And then, out of the blue, she hugged me.

"That's great," I told her. I caught my reflection in the refrigerator door handle. My hair was hanging in my eyes. I fussed with it. "Mom?"

"Hmm?"

"Am I pretty?" I asked.

She paused. "Doesn't your father always say so?"

"Yeah. But that's just Dad."

Mom feathered my bangs away from my eyes. She smiled. "Yes. You're pretty."

It felt weird, hearing Mom say it. Sort of like if Farley had said something like "Nice catch, Bird." Satisfied, I snatched a carrot to nibble on.

"By the way, that Lieutenant Peppel called for you," Mom said.

"Who?"

"The pilot who flour-bombed you. He joked that he needed to talk to you about a 'secret mission.' "

Then I remembered. He was talking about our deal!

"Bird. What are you up to?"

"Nothing," I told her.

Mom cocked her head at me and squinted her eyes. Uh-oh. When Mom got that look, she was tougher than Humphrey Bogart. She could practically x-ray through the best fibs you could ever think of.

"I'm just trying to get Margaret a date," I explained.

She wasn't buying it. I was sunk.

"Gosh. Can't I do something nice for my big sister?" I pleaded.

"I'm going to regret this, but you caught me in a good mood. All right."

"Thanks, Mom. How long until dinner?"

"About an hour—"

But I was already flying out the door.

Inside the airplane hangar, Lieutenant Peppel struggled to walk toward the wing of his P-40. It was like his parachute pack was way too heavy. And it was—because I was inside it. He checked the area and tried to climb onto the wing, bumping my head on the aileron.

"Ow!" I yelped.

"*Shhh!*" he scolded me.

Suddenly I heard another voice, that of the gruff old mechanic who worked on the planes there. The mechanic asked, "Taking her up again already, Lieutenant?"

"Uh, yeah. I wanted to flight-test that oil leak."

The mechanic must have noticed the trouble Lieutenant Peppel was having climbing onto the wing, because he got behind him and gave me a shove.

I yelped again.

"Was that you squawking?" the mechanic asked Lieutenant Peppel.

"Yeah, sorry," the lieutenant said. "I've got a . . . a weak kidney."

"That's 'cause you're bent over all wrong." The mechanic

shoved his knee into my butt and I had to clench my teeth to keep from hollering. "Here." He lifted the chute and rocked Lieutenant Peppel forward onto the wing. "I guess they forgot to teach you how to carry a chute in *college*, huh, flyboy?"

"Yeah, I reckon so," Lieutenant Peppel grumbled back. Then he whispered to me, "This better be worth it, Peach-pit."

The mechanic helped shove me down into the cramped cockpit. I was crumpled in a ball now and Lieutenant Peppel was basically sitting on my head.

"Thanks," the lieutenant said. "I got it from here."

"Okay," the mechanic said. He climbed down off the wing and pulled out the wheel chucks. I could hear him mutter as he walked away, "College boys."

As soon as he was gone, the lieutenant called out, "Okay, now."

I spilled out of the bottom of his chute pack and squeezed in behind the control stick, just in front of him. He strapped us both in while I stared reverently at the instruments sticking out on the control panel like jewels in a diamond mine. Beautiful.

"You're sure your sister will go out with me?"

I gave him a thumbs-up. "Affirmative."

I strapped on my helmet and watched carefully as Lieutenant Peppel checked his instruments.

"Mags on. Flaps set. Throttle set. Engine primed. Ready?"

I pulled down my goggles and squeezed my eyes shut.

"What's wrong?"

"I've never flown without my dad," I confessed. I couldn't believe it, but it had been almost six months since Dad and I had flown on my birthday.

"Don't you worry none. I'm first in my class."

I nodded excitedly and he spun up the flywheel and fired the engine over. The twelve cylinders pounded together in rhythm like a blazing boogie-woogie band and I smiled. It was the most wonderful sound I had ever heard. It shook your whole body, like the P-40 was just as anxious as we were to get off the ground and into the sky.

A moment later, the mighty fighter taxied out, S-turning toward the head of the runway. I popped my head up to see—and I was instantly splattered in the face with oil.

"Watch it." The lieutenant dragged me back down into the cockpit. "She's been blowing a little oil out of her stacks."

"*Now* you tell me." I coughed and spit out the oil, then wiped off my goggles. I looked over as we passed a T-6 trainer plane. The T-6 pilot did a double take and I realized that from his viewpoint, with me in the cockpit, it probably looked like Lieutenant Peppel had two heads. I quickly ducked back down.

"Power up," Lieutenant Peppel called out, and the engine started to scream. He stepped on the brakes with all his strength. Like a hound dog fighting his leash to chase the fox, the Warhawk tried to shake loose its brakes, eager to be airborne. "Here we go." Lieutenant Peppel released the brakes and had to stand on the rudder to keep us straight as the Warhawk tore off down the runway and carried us into the sky.

In a matter of minutes, we were over Geneseo, the Warhawk's massive propeller cutting through the clouds with ease as the lieutenant dipped and turned. Surrounded by the pillows of white, I felt like I was in heaven.

I had to yell to be heard over the engine. "What about your machine guns?"

"There's a trigger on the stick," the lieutenant hollered back. "But no bullets on account of this here being a trainer."

I reached down for a tempting red lever by my leg.

"Don't touch that!"

"What is it?" I asked.

"That's the bomb release."

"Flour?" I asked.

He nodded. "For target practice."

We made a high pass over the bay. I peered out the window. This was real. Me. In a P-40 Warhawk! If Dad could have seen me then, he wouldn't have believed it. I barely believed it myself.

"You really love flying, don't you?" the lieutenant said.

I nodded.

"Me too. Ever since I was no taller 'n you," he said. "The world seems gosh darn perfect from up here. All them houses in a row. Rivers bent around hills and trees all pretty much where they oughta be. Everything seems to fit together. When I'm flyin' in the clouds sometimes, it's hard to figure there's a war going on out there with folks trying to shoot our guys down."

"Yeah. Like my dad." I kind of dropped my head and the lieutenant wrapped his arms a little tighter around me.

"Sorry, Peach-pit. I forgot about your dad. He's a pilot?"

"The best. He taught me everything I know."

The lieutenant spoke close to my ear. "Ya know, kid, someday, if I have a daughter, I hope she loves flying as much as you."

"Yeah?"

"Yeah," he said.

"Thanks," I told him. He was a pretty nice guy, even if his takeoffs weren't near as smooth as Dad's. I almost felt sorry for siccing Margaret on him.

"Say, do you think your sister might like to go up for a ride? I could probably sneak her up in one of them old Kitty Hawks."

But before I could answer, my eye caught the outline of something black below the surface of the water in the bay. Oh my gosh, that was it! The sub!

"Lieutenant! Lieutenant! Look! Down in the bay."

"What?" he said.

"Tilt the wings!" I hollered.

He tilted the wings to see. "What is it? I don't see anything."

I looked down at the water, but of course by then it was gone. "Forget it," I said.

Then the lieutenant checked his watch and the setting sun and said, "We'd better get back. I'm not cleared for night flying."

I bit my lip and nodded okay. I guess it was gonna be up to Kenji and me to catch that spy sub.

It was Friday at noon when Kenji met me behind the oak tree in the playground. We firmed up our plans while we gobbled down our brown-bag lunches.

"We're all set for tonight," he said. "I got us four rocket flares, two Roman candles—"

"I saw the sub again," I interrupted him.

"What? When?"

"Lieutenant Peppel took me up in his Warhawk. That's when I spotted it in the bay," I said.

"Did *he* see it?"

Before I could answer, I noticed that crooked-toothed Farley Peck was making a beeline our way. "*Shhh.* We got company."

Farley walked right up to me and shoved me against the tree. "You dirty d-d-double-crossers. Where is he?"

"Who?" I asked.

"Who do you think, Birdbrain? My father."

"He's not in the tree house?" Kenji said.

With his other hand, Farley grabbed Kenji by the shirt. "Don't play dumb. Who did you t-t-tell?"

Across the playground, Principal Hartwig smelled trouble and started to head over.

I tried to loosen Farley's grip. "No one."

"He's probably just fishing or hiding out from the shore patrol or something," Kenji said, trying to pry himself free.

"If anything happens to him, you t-t-two are as good as d-d-dead," Farley stuttered.

Suddenly the strong hand of Principal Hartwig collared Farley. "What seems to be the problem?" The principal looked to me and Kenji for the answer.

"Nothing, Mr. Hartwig," I said.

Farley let go of Kenji. "Yeah, nothing."

"Good. Then how about you do your 'nothing' over there, Farley?"

"All right," he said. But before he was led away, Farley, with a deadly stare, whispered to us, "I better find him."

When I got home after school, Mom was dressed in a gray and white dress, standing over a pot of stew and trying to fasten a nurse's cap on her head.

"Red Cross tonight?" I asked.

"Mm-hmm," she answered. It seemed like Mom was volunteering for everything. She never used to, but Margaret said she was probably just keeping busy to keep her mind off Dad being gone.

"By the way, I've gotta go down to the bay and collect some stuff for school," I mentioned matter-of-factly.

"Not tonight," Mom said. "You're watching Alvin, remember?"

That was when my stomach sank into my shoes. I had

completely forgotten. "But, Mom! Can't Margaret do it? It's really important."

"Of course it is," she said, not really meaning it.

"No, I mean it. The fate of our country depends on it."

"I'm sure it does. But you'll have to work the 'fate of our country' out with Margaret. I have to help out at the hospital in half an hour." She took off her apron and handed me the spoon. "And keep stirring this."

As I took over stirring the stew, my little brother Alvin walked in.

"Reporting for duty," he said, saluting.

"Alvin!" Mom shrieked.

Alvin had given himself a crew cut with Margaret's scissors.

"When's Dad coming home?"

I'd sat Alvin down on the kitchen stool and was trying to even out his hair as best I could.

"Soon. Real soon," I told him.

"Are you sure?"

"He promised he would, didn't he?"

Alvin itched away some hair clippings that were dangling from the end of his nose. "Timmy Collins's dad isn't coming home. He died."

I stopped cutting. I had heard about Mr. Collins the day before. I petted Alvin's head. "I know."

"Timmy said his dad promised him he would come home."

I knelt down. "Hey. Remember how I told you last year, you could only climb in my bed if ten monsters came in your room?"

"Uh-huh."

"You can climb in my bed anytime you want. Okay?"

"Okay." He smiled. "All done, sir?"

I saluted him. "You're ready for duty, Private."

He tucked Mom's wooden spoon against his shoulder like a rifle and marched off to play in the backyard.

As soon as I got Alvin's hair clippings cleaned up, I hurried upstairs to the bedroom, where I found Margaret packing pajamas in her pillowcase for a slumber party. Was there anything dumber than Margaret and her girlfriends stuffing themselves with burnt popcorn and grape Nehi, playing records and giggling until all hours of the night about boys who were never gonna ask them out for a date anyway? I mapped out my strategy. Should I play up the close, unbreakable bond, which, Dad said, "only two sisters could ever know"?

Uh-uh. With no time to waste, I went right for the throat. "So. Friday night and no date again, huh?"

"Get lost, twerp."

There it was. Big-sisterly love in all its glory. It was time to spark her dull-witted interest. "Remember that cute lieutenant who was here a few weeks ago?"

Margaret played dumb, which wasn't hard. "Which one?"

"Um. The one who saw you in your bra."

Margaret walloped me in the face with her pillow. "What do you want this time?"

Maybe she wasn't so dumb. We could practically read each other's minds. "Just watch Alvin for me tonight."

"Forget it. I watched him last week," she said.

"Please. He'll go to bed early," I promised her. "Just have your party here."

"Why should I?"

"Because I've got a direct communication line to the lieutenant. He's very interested."

"Well, who said *I'm* interested?" Margaret said.

I dangled her pillow and flannel pajamas. "A slumber party on a Friday night? That pretty much says it all."

"Get lost," she said.

Maybe I had overplayed my hand? I glanced at her stack of icky *True Romance* magazines. The cover of one declared: "Confessions of a Jealous Lover!" That gave me an idea. I decided to try a new tactic.

"Of course, if you're not interested, I'm sure Betsy Brightwell could squeeze him onto her dance card."

Betsy had been a thorn in Margaret's side ever since fifth grade. Margaret had fallen hard for Billy Ackerman. She had spent that whole year doing everything she could think of to get Billy's attention. Every day, on the way to school, she would walk slowly in front of him, dropping her books, her handkerchief, even her lunch—anything that might provide an opportunity for her to flutter her eyelashes and ensnare him with her charms. But every time, Billy would just walk past her, chewing gum and obliviously tossing his baseball into his mitt. In desperation, Margaret had planned an elaborate "surprise" birthday party for herself. Billy ignored the invitation she'd sent him, and as the day grew near, Betsy volunteered to talk to him. She promised Margaret she knew a surefire way to get him to come to the party. The night of the party, to everyone's surprise, Billy indeed showed up—with the backstabbing Betsy on his arm, and a new leather mitt from Betsy's dad's hardware store stuffed in his jacket pocket.

"You wouldn't dare," Margaret said to me, fuming.

"Just try me." The thought of Betsy swooping in to snatch the lieutenant sent Margaret over the edge.

"Okay, okay. I'll do it. But if there's any trouble with Alvin, you're taking the blame."

I handed her back her pillow. "Deal."

An hour later, Kenji and I were walking along the south shore of the bay with an armful of fireworks and his Graflex camera.

"I figure our best shot is if we split up and light the bay from both sides." He handed me two Roman candles. "Take these and when I flash twice with my flashlight, light 'em."

"What about the noise?"

"I think these ones only flare."

"You *think*?" I said. I guess it had finally hit me that this wasn't some game. We were really gonna try and catch a spy. "Kenji?"

"Huh?"

"What's gonna happen if this works?" I asked.

"Then we get a picture of the spy sub."

"Yeah, but *then* what? Something tells me spies don't generally like having their picture taken."

Kenji swallowed hard. Then he tapped his fist against my shoulder to buck me up. "Hey. You want to get your dad home, don't you?"

I nodded.

"Just take your flashlight and signal me when you find a good spot," he said.

"Okay," I said, and headed for the north shore.

I was somewhere along the north shore, fumbling around in the grass for a dry spot to plant the flares, when I stepped through some brush and *thwump!* I tripped and fell flat on my face. I looked back and saw my ankle caught in a twist of boat line. When I pulled the line out of the sand and followed it, it led me to Father Krauss's boat. The boat was lying upside down in some weeds. I checked the hull for damage, but it seemed okay. So I crouched down to flip it over. I got a good grip on the rim. "One, two, three." I hoisted one side of the rowboat, and then *fwap!* A lifeless human arm plopped out.

"Ahhh!" I shrieked.

It was Mr. Peck, Farley's dad. His face and body were all pale and bloated with seawater. He was dead. I gasped for air but I was too frozen to scream out again. My arms went limp and I accidentally dropped the boat back onto Mr. Peck's dead, outstretched arm.

"Ahhh!" I screamed out again. I flashed my light across the bay to signal Kenji. I waited a moment until I saw his flashlight blink on and off, which let me know that he was coming. But it was a long way from him to me. And I didn't feel like staying there and keeping dead Mr. Peck company. I slowly backed away from the body. That was when I bumped right into something large and very *alive*.

I spun around. Oh God! In front of me was a towering man, dressed all in black, with a knit mask pulled over his face. But I could see his eyes. They were dark and empty, like a shark's. He grabbed me, lifting my feet off the ground, and covered my mouth so that I couldn't scream.

CHAPTER 11

Suddenly Kenji's flare lit up the moonless sky, surprising the man in black. With all my might I instinctively bit down hard into the forearm he had wrapped around my neck, and I didn't let go until I tasted blood.

The man screamed a strange word, *"Scheisse!"* I broke free and ran for my life.

At last I was able to scream out, "Kenji!"

Across the bay, I could see the beam of Kenji's flashlight dancing through the grass as he ran to find me. I heard him calling out. "Bird?"

But I was busy running blindly through the high marsh weeds because I could hear the splash of pounding boot-steps gaining on me.

"Help, help!" I screamed between gasps. I tumbled into some thick brush, scraping my arms, and then somehow I managed to scramble up a tree. Within seconds, the man in black was below me. I had to cover my mouth with my hands and hold my breath to keep from screaming.

About thirty yards downshore, I could hear Kenji running full speed. Without breaking stride, he reached over his head and fired his last flare. It rocketed into the sky like a shooting star. When the flare burst overhead, it lit up the bay.

Immediately, the man in black ducked behind my tree. I could tell he sensed I was nearby. In a dark, out-of-breath whisper he called out, "You're such a clever little girl, Bird."

How on earth did he know my name? My left leg, which was supporting me on a branch, started to shake. I tried to steady it with my hands, but it kept right on shaking.

"I bet you're clever enough to forget everything you saw tonight. That is, if you like your family *alive*." He sniffed the air like a bloodhound and checked his watch. "I know you can hear me."

Suddenly, my stupid quivering leg slipped free and snapped a branch.

"Well, well," the killer snickered. Slowly, his gaze moved upward.

But before he saw me, he was blinded by a ghost-white beam of light from the bay. A fishing boat was approaching the shore.

"Who's-a there?"

It was Mr. Ramponi, calling out from his boat! He shined his spotlight into the woods.

The man in black ducked down. He looked up at me and said, "I know you'll keep our secret, for your family's sake." And then he slowly disappeared into the shadows of the woods.

Then Kenji's voice cried out from ten yards away, "Bird? Bird!"

I slid down from the tree, barely able to stand on my wobbly legs.

Kenji burst through the darkness. "Are you okay, Bird? What happened?"

But before I could open my mouth, a deafening explosion ripped through the air, rattling our bones and sending shock waves through the earth beneath our feet. I grabbed on to Kenji and fell to the ground.

My ears were pounding and everything sounded muffled, like my head had been stuffed with cotton. Were we being bombed? I tried, but I couldn't hear any plane engines overhead. I braced for more explosions, but they didn't come.

By the time we struggled back to our feet and dusted ourselves off, a giant cloud of smoke and flames was beginning to fill the sky from somewhere inland.

110

"Who's-a there?" Mr. Ramponi cried out again.

Kenji was about to call out when I slapped my hand over his mouth. With the killer's threat against my family fresh in my mind, I shook him and whispered, "Listen. If anyone asks, we weren't here tonight. And we didn't see anything. All right?"

"But I *didn't* see anything," Kenji said.

"Just cross your heart and promise!"

"All right. I promise." He traced a cross on his chest. "Cross my heart."

I crossed mine, too, and held out my pinky to seal the pledge. "Hope to die."

He clasped my pinky but looked at me like he wasn't really sure. "Hope to die."

The next morning it was raining like crazy, but that didn't stop me and half the town from finding our way out to the exploded P-40 engine factory. The only time I had seen this many people standing outside in the rain was after Farley's little brother Frankie fell in the bay and drowned two summers ago. But stuff like buildings blowing up just didn't happen in Geneseo. A huge chunk of the factory's redbrick wall was missing, completely blown away. It looked like a tank had run through it. Through the hole I could see that inside, the main engine-block casting oven was no more.

Outside, ignoring the steady downpour, Deputy Steyer and a team of soldiers were painstakingly searching through the ashes and smoldering debris when a big, black Buick Roadmaster pulled up. It wasn't the kind of car you saw around town. It looked like something out of a gangster movie. When the door opened, out stepped a tall, clean-cut man in a trench coat. His face was half hidden by the brim of his hat.

The deputy approached him. "Fred Steyer. I'm the town deputy." They shook hands.

"FBI Special Agent Barson," I heard the tall man say.

FBI? Holy smokes! Well, that was good, right? They'd find the man in black and I wouldn't have to say anything, and Margaret, Alvin, and Mom would be safe.

The deputy showed him some of the debris. Then a second agent handed Mr. Barson something that looked like a melted alarm clock.

"Was anyone killed?" Agent Barson asked.

Deputy Steyer nodded solemnly. "Two people. The main casting oven exploded at about eight-thirty last night. We checked the gas lines, but they seem okay."

Agent Barson stopped. He knelt down and peeled off a piece of plastic that was melted onto a piston rod. He smelled it. Then he stood up and very slowly shook his head.

"This was no accident," he told Deputy Steyer. He looked out over the crowd of people, and I could see his eyes for the first time. They were sharp and focused, almost more triangular than round. They tracked and darted from side to side, like the eyes of Wendy's cat when it was stalking a sparrow. Then he stared right at me.

"Somebody knows something," he said to the deputy. "You can't hide in a town this small."

"Deputy Steyer?" A man hollered from the deputy's car. "You've got a call to go to the bay. They said they've found Ben Peck."

I felt a sick twist in my stomach and turned away. This wasn't how things were supposed to turn out. Kenji and I were supposed to be heroes.

"Who is he?" Agent Barson asked.

"A draft dodger. Disappeared about a month ago," the deputy told him.

"Let's go," Agent Barson said.

By the time I got to the north shore, Deputy Steyer and several fishermen were carrying the body of Mr. Peck to an ambulance.

Agent Barson stopped the stretcher. He reached down and lifted the sheet. "Killed with one stab wound. Not the work of an amateur. Looks like your draft dodger got in the wrong person's way."

Suddenly Farley came running out of the woods. His face was all red, and he was huffing and puffing like he'd run all the way from town. He tried to reach the stretcher, but several fishermen held him back.

"Let me see!" he cried.

"It's his father," Deputy Steyer explained to Agent Barson.

Agent Barson looked at Farley a moment. Then he said, "Let him go."

Farley stepped up to the body. He grabbed hold of the sheet. But at the last minute he couldn't look. He turned his head away. Before last night, the only dead body I had ever seen was my great-grandfather Alvin. He had looked nice and peaceful, almost like he was sleeping in the casket. When I saw Mr. Peck under that boat, he didn't look peaceful. He looked like a dead animal on the road. If it had been my dad under that sheet, I wouldn't have looked, either.

Agent Barson knelt down next to Farley. "Someone sabotaged the plane factory last night. I think your father tried to stop him." He put his arm around Farley's shoulder, but Farley stiffened and knocked it away. "Who else knew he was living in the woods?" the agent asked.

Farley lifted his head and his eyes locked with mine. I didn't know what he was thinking, but I knew that if I got dragged into this now, the man in black was gonna come after my family for sure. Farley looked like a volcano about to explode with anger. He spit out one word.

"Kenji."

At the sound of my friend's name, I heard others in the crowd start to grumble: "I knew it." "Of course."

Agent Barson looked at the deputy, who explained, "A Japanese boy. Just moved here. He lives in town with his uncle."

The rained-on crowd started to fidget and the air around

me suddenly got this weird sort of scary electricity. It was like on the playground when all the kids were gathered around Farley and whoever he was picking on, and everyone was just waiting, almost wanting someone to throw that first punch.

"Let's find him," Agent Barson said. "Before some of these townspeople do."

They piled into the black Roadmaster and drove away.

CHAPTER 12

"This is asking for trouble, Bird," Mom said.

"What's new?" Margaret broke in. "She's had an open invitation for trouble stamped across her face since she was two."

"But he doesn't have anyone else," I said.

Agent Barson was waiting with Kenji by his parked car in our dirt driveway. I stole a glance at Kenji through our front window. He looked different. He wasn't the same kid who'd saved me from drowning when the sub tipped our boat, or the kid who'd come running to my rescue when the man in black had me up a tree. Somehow he looked, I don't know, smaller.

"His uncle's in jail. Agent Barson said Kenji needs a place to stay," I told Mom.

"That's not our responsibility," Mom said.

"Neither is the Widow Gorman, and we help her."

Mom was avoiding looking out the window at Kenji. She knew I was right, at least partially. I think she was just afraid.

"It's not the same," she said.

So I pulled out my trump card. "Dad would let him stay."

"That's not fair," she said.

Maybe not, but it seemed to tip the scales in Kenji's favor.

"He won't eat much," I promised. "Just look at him. He's not much bigger than his suitcase."

Finally Mom started to bend. "I don't want to hear about any more sea monsters or submarines."

"Okay," I agreed.

"The first sign of trouble and he's got to leave," she said.

"Deal," I told her as I burst out the door to tell Kenji. Agent Barson carried his suitcase and I led him inside.

"Thank you, ma'am," Agent Barson said to my mom.

Kenji stopped and turned to the agent. "You know my uncle didn't do it."

Agent Barson soaked in Kenji's stare, and Mom and I led Kenji upstairs toward Alvin's room.

"You'll have to share a room with my little brother," I said.

"That's okay," Kenji said.

As we opened the door, Mom let out a gasp. "Alvin!"

"Surprise?" mumbled Alvin. My wacky little brother had Margaret's bra strapped to his head like a skullcap.

Kenji looked at me and we all burst out laughing.

"Come with me, Captain Alvin." Mom escorted him out.

Thank God for my little brother. It was the first smile any of us had had all day.

Later, after Mom had gone, I pumped Kenji for the details of what had happened.

"The deputy and the FBI guy just barged right in," he told me. "My uncle asked, 'What are you doing?' And then Deputy Steyer started rummaging through everything. He found a Japanese flag buried in one of Uncle Tomo's drawers. Then they asked where he was last night at eight-thirty. My uncle said he heard the noise, and he asked if something had happened at the factory. They got real suspicious when he said that. So I told them he was home, with me."

"Good thinking," I said.

"But they didn't believe me."

"But you didn't say *we* were by the bay, did you?" I asked, panicked.

"No. I didn't say anything about the bay. But my uncle wouldn't let me cover for him anyway. He said he wasn't home, but instead had gone to visit someone after work. Then the G-man found my uncle's gunpowder and fuse materials."

"Oh no!"

"I tried to explain that they were for the Fourth of July, to make fireworks. But then they found something else in my uncle's toolbox. They said it was some kind of special explosive, like what they found at the factory. My uncle tried to tell them it wasn't his, that he didn't know how it got there, but they didn't believe him. Then the deputy put him in handcuffs and said he was arresting him for the sabotage of the Warhawk engine factory, and the murder of Mr. Peck." Then Kenji leaned in closer to me and whispered, "Is that what you saw last night? Mr. Peck, dead?"

I nodded. "That's why I screamed." It was kind of the truth.

"Why the heck didn't you tell me?"

"I . . . couldn't." It wasn't much of an explanation, but he seemed to accept it for the time being.

"Anyway. After that, they roped off our apartment like it was some crime scene and said I'd have to find another place to stay."

He started to shake a little. Suddenly all the toughness I'd seen when he whacked that home run against Farley seemed to melt away. Now he looked as scared as I felt inside. I put my hand on Kenji's shoulder and he started to cry.

After supper I offered to help Mom with the dishes, and when I started, Kenji slipped out onto the porch. He'd been real quiet all through the meal and had eaten hardly anything, not even my mom's chocolate pudding.

After a little while Mom nudged me. "Go on. I can finish these," she said.

I dried my hands off and went outside.

The night was dark, with just a tiny sliver of moon to light the sky. Kenji seemed to be someplace far away, gazing out across our backyard. He looked lost, like the Widow Gorman did whenever someone mentioned her son, Charlie.

I sat down next to Kenji. "I'm really sorry about your uncle Tomo," I said.

Kenji turned toward me. "What happened last night, Bird? Can you finger the mug who really killed Mr. Peck?"

"I . . . I can't tell you," I said.

"Why not?"

"I just can't." The last thing he needed was the man in black coming after him, too.

He looked at me, kind of hurt. "I thought we were friends."

"We are." I wished I could tell him the truth. That I was only trying to protect him and everybody else from the real killer. And that he was probably the best friend I'd ever had. Even better than Wendy. I wished I could tell him that I thought he was ten times tougher than Farley Peck and as good a dancer as Fred Astaire any day of the week. But those were the kinds of things, like telling obnoxious Margaret that I loved her, that never seemed to find their way out of my mouth.

"Baloney," he said. "You think my uncle did it. Just because he's Japanese."

"No, I don't," I told him. "But I can't say anything. Not until my dad comes home." That was the plan I'd come up with while lying in bed the night before.

"Can't you do anything without your dad?" Kenji said.

"He'll be home on leave in July," I said, with hope. "My dad will know what to do." I figured that as long as I kept my mouth shut, everyone would be safe until then.

Kenji kicked the porch post in frustration. "I wish *my* parents could come home."

I didn't know what to say. There was a long silence. Nothing but crickets and bullfrogs chirping and croaking at each other. Then I finally got it.

"Your parents aren't really dead, are they?" I asked.

He shook his head like he was sick of pretending. "They're in a prison camp in California."

"Prison?" I would have never guessed that in a million years. "For what?"

"Being Japanese," he said matter-of-factly.

"I don't believe it."

"Believe it," he said.

Just then, at the end of the driveway, Lieutenant Peppel and Margaret pulled up on the lieutenant's motor scooter.

I lowered my voice a little. "Kenji. This is America."

"Not if you look like me," Kenji said.

I assumed he was telling the truth, but I still didn't

121

understand. How could they put his parents in jail just because they were Japanese? We watched Margaret and the lieutenant climb off the motor scooter and then steal a kiss good night. It felt funny, as if we shouldn't have been looking, and Kenji scooted away from me a little like he was afraid I might try and smooch him or something. I shrugged it off and wondered out loud about his parents.

"It's not fair," I said. "Just because you're a little different."

"What do you mean, *different*?" Kenji said, suddenly angry. "I'm no different than you."

I thought it over. "Yeah. I guess it's kind of like me wanting to be a fighter pilot."

But Kenji looked at me like I just didn't get it. "It's not like that at all."

A night wind shook the trees. After a while I got the courage to ask him, "How did you sneak out? Of the prison camp, I mean?"

"I didn't sneak out. After Pearl Harbor, stuff started to happen. Someone threw a brick through our window. Then they cut up a bunch of my dad's fishing nets. So my parents packed me up and shipped me away to some friends of theirs in St. Louis. Like their lousy record player, or that stupid camera. When they heard that only Japanese on the West Coast would have to go to camps, they had me sent here to Geneseo, to my uncle."

"Why didn't they come, too?"

" 'Cause they cared more about losing their house and fishing boat than they did about me, that's why."

"You lost your house?"

"That's what my uncle said. When President Roosevelt signed the executive order, they had two days to sell everything they owned. All my stuff—toys, comics, movie posters—it's all gone."

"You must miss your parents."

He rubbed his eyes, then looked away. "Not much."

"Have you heard from them?" I asked.

"They've written. I guess."

Then I remembered. "Those cut-open letters on your uncle's shelf?"

"The government opened them. I'm not gonna read them. Ever."

Behind us, from inside the kitchen, Mom started singing along with a wartime love song on the radio. I had never realized it, but she had a really pretty voice.

"I'm sure they didn't want to send you away," I told him. "Maybe they did it to protect you?"

"If you loved someone, would you send them away?" he asked.

I tried to imagine being sent to prison with my family. If I could have saved my dad from prison, would I have had the guts to send him away?

"Only if I loved them a real lot," I said.

The next day was Sunday. With a little begging and pleading, I convinced Mom to take Kenji along with us to church. I knew God was busy with the war, listening to prayers for all the soldiers and stuff like that. Father Krauss had explained that God answered every prayer, only sometimes the answer was no, or not yet. So I wasn't expecting any miracles. But it made me feel better, telling my troubles to someone. And next to Dad, God was the best listener I knew.

We were a little late, thanks to Margaret and her *hair*, and as we approached the chapel I could hear Father Krauss addressing the congregation from the pulpit. His voice was strong and deep. I always loved the way it echoed like it was floating just above your head.

"Jesus said to the crowd that had gathered, 'Happy are the kind and merciful, for they shall be shown mercy.' "

As we climbed up the church steps, my mind drifted off to thoughts about Dad and how much easier it would have been to walk in behind him right then.

The vestibule door creaked open and Father Krauss seemed pleasantly surprised to see us walking down the aisle. But as soon as all the parishioners saw Kenji, a wave of whispering and gossip washed through the crowd.

Father Krauss ignored the mumbling and carried on. "And Jesus said, 'Happy are those who are persecuted because they are good, for the Kingdom of Heaven is theirs.' "

I took hold of Kenji's hand and we found our way to a half-filled pew near the front. I whispered to Mr. and Mrs. Lashley, "Excuse me, could you slide down?"

When they turned to see me with Kenji, they snatched up Minnie's hand and shuffled to another pew in disgust. As

124

Mom, Margaret, and Alvin filed in next to us, all the people in the surrounding pews moved to other areas like we had some sort of disease.

Then Father Krauss got a stern look in his eye. The same kind of look he gave me when I called Freddie Brooks "fatso" after he stole my place in line for Communion. Father Krauss shut his Bible kind of loudly and everyone got real quiet. His eyes scanned the whole congregation, and when he finally spoke, his voice penetrated everyone.

"And he said, 'Happy are the *just*, for they shall be judged fairly.' The Book of Exodus reminds us all, 'Never falsely charge a stranger with evil; for remember, you yourselves were strangers in the land of Egypt.' " He smiled at me and Kenji. Bowed his head. "And *that*, brothers and sisters, is the word of the Lord."

CHAPTER

13

It was another month or so before Uncle Tomo's trial started, on July 3. I had never actually been inside the Geneseo courthouse before. It was just a redbrick building with some pretty white pillars out front, but there was something about it that made you feel like you had better tell the truth inside or the walls would know you were lying.

From the front steps, a crowd of townspeople and strangers spilled out of the packed entryway. Mom, Alvin, Margaret, and I squeezed by. There were supposed to be some newspapermen here who'd come up all the way from

New York City. A bunch of the local paperboys were all trying to impress them by loudly hawking the local headline: JAP SABOTEUR GOES ON TRIAL.

Inside, the district attorney, Mr. Lashley, combed his hair and straightened his tie. He was Minnie's dad—something she had to mention at least once a day. In church and around town, he and Mrs. Lashley pretty much always pretended like we were invisible, except when he needed Dad to fix his stupid car. I looked at him and wondered why he hadn't had to go and fight the war. Two bits says he was probably scared, like Farley's dad.

Mr. Lashley winked at the reporters in the gallery. Then he turned to Uncle Tomo's lawyer, Mr. Wylie, and they laughed like schoolmates about something while Kenji was sworn in. Mr. Wylie was the public defender. Mom told me that meant he was the lawyer who the government hired because Uncle Tomo couldn't find anybody willing to defend him. It was kind of screwy, because if Uncle Tomo's lawyer worked for the government, and the district attorney worked for the government, and the judge worked for the government, who was on Uncle Tomo's side?

Mr. Wylie was a little younger than Mr. Lashley, but he looked about ten years older on account of his hair—or rather, his lack of it. The little bit of hair he did have started on one side and draped over to the other, sort of like a Christmas ribbon on a bowling ball. It was hard to believe that the balding, shiny-headed Mr. Wylie and the poufy-haired Mrs. Lashley were actually brother and sister.

Judge Dickens sat at his raised desk, twirling his wispy gray eyebrows and fanning himself to keep cool. He was a big man, with a stomach-rattling grumble of a voice that he liked to show off by singing "Good King Wenceslas" every year at the Christmas pageant. I was always a little afraid of him when he dressed up as Santa Claus, but Dad said he had honest eyes.

Kenji's uncle Tomo sat with the deputy directly behind him. Not more than ten feet away, I saw Farley Peck, looking meaner than I had ever seen him before. I guess he had a good reason, for once. After all, somebody had killed his dad. But he was just too dumb—as usual—to see that they had the wrong guy. I squeezed into the front row of spectators with Mom, Margaret, Alvin, and Agent Barson.

After a lot of talking and announcements about "case number something or other" and "the State versus Fujita this and that," District Attorney Lashley and Mr. Wylie made their opening statements. Mr. Lashley's was a lot louder and longer and more boring. When it was the public defender's turn, Mr. Wylie just stood up and said that Mr. Tomo might have had motive and opportunity, but the DA still had to prove he was guilty beyond a reasonable doubt.

It was late in the afternoon by the time the DA called his first witness: "FBI Special Agent Barson."

Agent Barson walked up and sat in that chair with the low fence around it. Mr. Lashley asked Agent Barson a lot of technical-sounding questions about the factory, and about the chemicals that are used to make bombs, and about the explosives that the agent and Deputy Steyer had found in Uncle Tomo's apartment. Then Mr. Lashley was done. He nodded and politely turned the questioning over to Mr. Wylie, who asked just one question.

"Agent Barson, Mr. Fujita explained to you that he makes fireworks to sell for the Fourth of July celebration. Aren't the explosives you found simply the materials used for fireworks?"

Agent Barson thought about it for a moment. Then he said firmly, "Not unless you wanted to level half of Main Street."

Funny thing was, Mr. Wylie didn't seem that surprised. He just straightened his tie and said, "Thank you."

It was then, when Judge Dickens excused Agent Barson and Mr. Lashley stood up and called his next witness, that I got a sick feeling in my stomach.

"Farley Peck," the DA said.

That awful name sounded even worse when a grown-up said it in court. What did Farley know about Uncle Tomo? Nothing. Whatever he was up to, I was darn sure it meant trouble for Kenji, his uncle, and me. When Farley walked past, he made sure to step on my foot.

"Ow," I said under my breath.

Farley sat down in the witness box, the area with the wooden fence around it. There's something not right about having a fence indoors. It looked like the same kind of fence they used to hold the prizewinning hog in at the county fair. And Farley was still wearing his stupid overalls! In court, in front of the newspapermen and everybody. What was wrong with him? Didn't he know you're supposed to dress up when you're in court in front of the judge? All the ladies in town would have blamed his sloppy appearance on his mom, only they couldn't 'cause she had left Farley's dad and run off with some shoe salesman who came through town four years ago.

"Do you swear to tell the truth, the whole truth, and nothing but the truth, so help you God?" the bailiff asked.

Farley shrugged. "Sure."

"Just say, 'I do,' son," Judge Dickens told him.

"I do, son," Farley said. Everybody laughed at that, and that made Farley scowl.

"Now, son, where were you on the night of the explosion?" District Attorney Lashley asked.

"I was walking out of the woods. I had just brought some food to my daddy."

"You mean your father, Ben Peck, who had been living in the woods?"

"Yep."

"What happened to your father?"

That was when Farley stood up and pointed straight at Uncle Tomo. "*He* killed him."

"That's a lie!" Kenji jumped up and hollered.

"Silence!" the judge said. You could see that Kenji's outburst made him mad. "Young man, you will sit down and keep silent, or you will be forced to leave. I will not have my courtroom turned into a circus." He nodded at Mr. Lashley. "You may continue, prosecutor."

"Son, did you see him kill your father?" Mr. Lashley touched Farley's shoulder like you would if you thought someone was gonna cry, only this was more like he was pretending he thought Farley was gonna cry. Like he was acting.

But Farley shucked away his hand anyway. "I seen him running away from the factory and into the woods just before the factory blew up. Next day, they found my daddy with a knife in his back. That's how I know that Jap done it."

"He's lying!" Kenji burst out. "He wasn't even in the woods that night. We would have seen him."

"We?" Mr. Lashley said.

"Shut up, Kenji," I shushed him. But it was too late. The lawyers went up and talked with the judge for about ten minutes. When they were done, Farley was dismissed and a new witness was called to the stand.

"Kenji Fujita."

Kenji got up. He looked at me. I shook my head. He turned around and marched to the witness box.

The bailiff held up the Bible. "Do you swear to tell the truth, the whole truth, and nothing but the truth, so help you God?"

Kenji nodded. "I do."

He was so short you could barely see him over the fence of the witness box, so after they swore him in, they had him sit on a briefcase. Then the district attorney approached with his first question. "Ken-ji, huh? Exactly what kind of name is that?"

"I don't know. My name?" Kenji looked puzzled.

"Behave yourself, prosecutor," said Judge Dickens.

"Was there some sort of objection, Your Honor?" Mr. Lashley asked real innocently, like he didn't know what the judge was talking about.

"No objection from me," Mr. Wylie answered.

"Well, there ought to be," the judge barked. Then he looked sternly at Mr. Wylie. "Listen to me, Felix. Either you defend this man properly, or I'll call a mistrial faster than you can say William Jennings Bryan."

Mr. Wylie straightened his strand of hair. "Of course, Your Honor."

"Now get on with it," Judge Dickens said.

District Attorney Lashley started over. "Thank you, Your Honor. Now Ken-ji, your uncle, Mr. Fujita, keeps explosives in the house, doesn't he?"

"Just fireworks," Kenji said.

"Just fireworks. Uh-huh. What were you doing when the explosion occurred at the Warhawk engine factory?"

I bit my lip and shook my head again at Kenji. He paused a second, then blurted out, "We had just shot off some flares by the bay."

"We," again? *Oh no! He's done it now.*

"You mean, you and your uncle?" Mr. Lashley asked.

Kenji looked at me. "No. Me and a friend."

"Oh. Do you mean Bird McGill?" Mr. Lashley trumpeted.

Suddenly it felt like everyone's eyes had pounced on me. I wanted to crawl under my chair. It was even worse than that time in the third-grade spelling bee finals when I ended *Mississippi* with a *y*. Mom turned to me, too, but I just looked down at my shoes.

"Do you mean Bird McGill?" the DA repeated.

"I guess so," Kenji answered.

"So you and Bird were playing with your uncle's explosives?" the DA said with a smirk.

"No. Just some flares. You know, Roman candles. We needed enough light . . . to take a picture."

Mr. Lashley looked suddenly interested. "What *picture*?"

Kenji mumbled, knowing full well they would never believe it. "Of the submarine we saw."

"Submarine?" The DA dropped his jaw, like a circus clown would if he was pretending to be shocked.

Mr. Wylie snorted, struggling to contain his laughter. It was like one of Farley's dumb fart noises in school. It wasn't really funny, but when one person started laughing, it was contagious. The rest of the spectators heard Mr. Wylie's snort and started to scoff and snicker.

Judge Dickens pounded his gavel. "Mr. Wylie, you are begging for a contempt citation."

Mr. Wylie cleared his throat and tried to put on a serious expression. "It won't happen again, Your Honor."

The DA approached the jury, jingling the change in his pocket like he wouldn't have believed Kenji in a million years. "Where is this 'picture' of a submarine?"

"Well . . ." Kenji lowered his head. "The factory blew up before we got a chance to take it."

"Of course it did." Mr. Lashley grinned. "No further questions, Your Honor."

Then Kenji jumped to his feet. "But it was in the bay! Bird and I saw it. It knocked over our rowboat!"

Mr. Lashley called out louder, this time sounding out each word like a kindergarten teacher repeating something for the tenth time, "No. Further. Questions. Your Honor."

Kenji cried out, "He didn't do it. He didn't kill Mr. Peck. Ask Bird. She knows who did it!"

Oh no! Why'd he have to say that?

"That's enough, son," the judge said, growing angrier. "Your testimony is finished."

The crowd grew unruly. Once again all their eyes turned to me. I felt a chill, and I knew that somewhere, somehow, in that courtroom, the man in black was watching me right then.

The judge pounded his gavel again and checked his watch. "This trial will reconvene the day after tomorrow, after the July Fourth holiday."

Mom took hold of me. "Bird. What is Kenji talking about?"

"I don't know," I said, hoping like crazy she couldn't tell I was lying.

134

Terrified, I grabbed Kenji as he walked past and pulled him into a corner. I shook him. "I told you not to say anything until my dad comes home."

"It'll be too late," Kenji pleaded. "My uncle needs your help now."

From the back of the crowd, Farley shot us an angry look, and I knew things were only gonna get worse from there on in.

The next night, I was lying awake in my bed holding a small American flag as the last of the July Fourth fireworks exploded in the Widow Gorman's backyard down the hill. After years of saying "H, E, double-L, no!" the Widow Gorman had finally let the town use her cornfield for the show. But even though I knew Dad was off somewhere fighting for our freedom, I didn't feel much like going to the fireworks that year. And with Kenji staying at our house and the trial and everything, Mom had figured it would be best if we just watched them from home. Mom had made sandwiches and potato salad, but I didn't eat much. Not because it wasn't good. I just had too much on my mind.

What was I going to say at the trial? The man in black had said that if I told them about him, he'd hurt my family. No one would believe me anyway. What was the point? But if I didn't tell them, then Kenji would look like a fool and a liar. And it'd be Farley's word against Kenji's and Uncle Tomo's. There didn't seem to be any way out. Unless . . .

Maybe they wouldn't call me to the stand? Why would they bother? They had laughed at Kenji when he told them about the sub and the picture. Who wants to hear the crackpot ramblings of a weirdo kid like me who memorizes fighter plane manuals and sees sea monsters and submarines? Yeah, what was I worrying about? They probably wouldn't even call me to the stand.

So instead of thinking about the trial and Kenji, and my dad, and the man in black, I decided to distract myself into falling asleep by dreaming up ways to smother my snoring sister Margaret. She sounded like a congested water buffalo.

Then I heard: *"Shhh!"* "Stop flapping your trap." It was several boys' voices whispering outside my window. I couldn't catch all of what they were saying, but the loudest one kept stuttering, like you-know-who. "Gimme that. You want them to hear you, s-s-s-stupid?"

Before I could get out of bed and to the window, there was the crackle of a match and the next thing I knew, one of our upstairs windows shattered like someone had thrown a brick through it.

"Hey! Come back here!" I hollered at three or four shadowy figures running into the darkness.

"For gosh sakes, Bird. Who're you yelling at?" Margaret joined me at the window. But they were gone.

Then, as we leaned out our window, we both noticed the orange flickering coming from Alvin's window.

"Fire!" Margaret shouted.

But her voice was drowned out by a rapid-fire flurry of *BANG!* and *POP!* that sounded like bombs and gunshots.

We raced into Alvin's room just as the curtains caught fire. A string of firecrackers exploded and danced among the flames on the floor. The smoke was already making it hard to see and breathe. Poor little Alvin was cocooned in his blanket, screaming, "Mommy, Mommy!" Kenji dragged him out from under the covers.

"Watch out for the broken glass!" I warned him. Kenji threw my little brother over his shoulder like a carpet roll and dodged the glass splinters as Margaret shoved the three of us out the door. She stayed behind, trying to smother the flames with a blanket.

"Is everyone all right?" Mom yelled as she collided with us in the hall.

Kenji and I nodded, coughing. Mom uncovered Alvin, kissed him, and grabbed me hard, by the shoulders. "Take Alvin and Kenji downstairs, now!"

The last thing I saw before running down the stairs was Mom and Margaret ripping Alvin's choo-choo-train curtains down and using his blanket to try and smother the flames that had already engulfed the German cuckoo clock that used to be Grandpa McGill's.

The thing was, I'd always hated that cuckoo clock. It never kept the right time and always got stuck *cuckoo*ing, over and over, every Saturday morning until Dad would silence it with a screwdriver. But it was strange to see my house on fire. Even the things I used to hate about it were suddenly the things I wanted desperately to save. Two hours after the fire started, I sat wrapped in a blanket on our front lawn, staring at the upstairs of our wonderful, drafty yellow farmhouse, which was now stained black from the fire. Principal Hartwig and the other volunteer firemen, along with Lieutenant Peppel's squadron from the base, had formed a bucket line and managed to put out the fire. Margaret rocked Alvin and sang to him softly, trying to get him to fall back asleep.

Mom and Deputy Steyer packed Kenji's stuff into the police car. Kenji sat in the backseat looking pale and pretty scared. I was scared, too. Someone had tried to burn our house down. I couldn't prove it, of course, but I knew it was Farley.

"It'll be safer for everyone with Kenji at the station," said the deputy.

"But Dad will be home next week," I protested to Mom. Maybe it didn't make sense, but the truth was, I felt safer having Kenji around. He was the only person on my side.

Mom knelt down by me. "Bird. Remember our deal? Wouldn't you say this qualifies as trouble?"

I shrugged. "I guess so."

"Not to mention, your father would never forgive me if I let anything happen to you."

"It's really for the best, Mrs. McGill," Deputy Steyer said.

I tried to believe them. But making Kenji go was like letting the bad guys win. It wasn't Kenji's fault we were at war, any more than it was Farley's or Father Krauss's or Mr. Ramponi's. Was I the only one who could see that?

The next day was the hottest day of the summer. All the lady jurors fanned themselves with their straw hats while the men broke down and loosened their ties and shirt collars. Kenji had to sit up front with Deputy Steyer.

I made sure we got there late so that Mom and I would have to sit in the balcony. After the excitement of the fire, Mom had decided it would be best for Margaret to stay home with Alvin until the trial was over.

Judge Dickens called the court to order. "Your next witness, prosecutor?"

I held my breath and doubled-crossed my fingers, just like when I didn't want Mrs. Simmons to call me to the blackboard.

"Tomo Fu-jita." It worked!

Uncle Tomo got up slowly and walked to the stand. He looked small, and old, and I could tell he was uncomfortable with all the people staring at him. There was something different about the way the DA questioned Uncle Tomo, too. Mr. Lashley didn't even bother trying to be polite to Uncle Tomo, as he had with the other witnesses. He started out asking Uncle Tomo the same simple questions over and over. It was like he was talking to a child and trying to catch him in a lie.

Then, all of a sudden, the DA just blurted out, "Mr. Fu-jita. Why did you kill Mr. Peck?"

Uncle Tomo looked surprised. So did the judge and everyone else.

"I not kill him. I not kill anyone."

"Why did you sabotage the factory?" the DA asked.

"I not sabotage the factory."

"Where were you the night of the explosion?"

Uncle Tomo paused. "I visit someone."

"Your accomplice?"

"No. Makiko."

"And who or what is Ma-ki-ko?"

"My wife."

"Really." Mr. Lashley rolled his eyes for the jury. "Does your wife live in the woods?"

"In cemetery. She die, on the boat to America."

I think that must have made Mr. Lashley a little uncomfortable, because he quickly changed the subject. "So, when you left the cemetery, is that when you ran into Farley Peck?"

Uncle Tomo shook his head. "I never see boy. When factory explode, I run home to find my nephew."

"Mr. Fujita, why would this boy Farley, whose father was murdered, lie?"

Because that's what Farley does, I wanted to say. Everybody knew that. I'd known it since the first day of kindergarten, when Farley told me his dad used to be President of the United States.

"Perhaps he want someone to blame," Uncle Tomo said. "I understand this."

"You *understand*. How thoughtful of you." That was when Mr. Lashley walked over to the evidence table. He unfolded a large flag. It was white, with a big bloodred circle in the center.

"Do you recognize this, Mr. Fu-jita?"

Everyone in the courtroom knew what it was.

"It is flag of Japan," Uncle Tomo said.

That was when I saw Uncle Tomo's attorney, Mr. Wylie, take a drink of water and wink at Mr. Lashley.

"According to the police report, this flag was found in your home," Mr. Lashley said. "Who does it belong to?"

Uncle Tomo paused and looked over at the jury. He held his head up. "It is mine." His answer set off grumbles throughout the gallery. Then Uncle Tomo added, "But I have American flag, too."

The DA scoffed, pretending he didn't hear the last part.

So he had a Japanese flag? So what? He grew up in Japan. His parents and grandparents lived in Japan. But he hadn't been back there for years. If I moved to some faraway country, maybe I'd keep an American flag to remind me of my old country, too.

"Mr. Fu-jita, how long have you lived in our country?"

"I here twenty years."

"That's a long time. Are you a citizen of this country?" asked the DA.

"No." Uncle Tomo got a sad look on his face. His head dropped a little. "Not allowed."

"Really?" Mr. Lashley smiled and shook his head like

he was saying "shame on you" to a child. "And why is that?"

"Japanese not allowed," Uncle Tomo said. "Unless born here, like my nephew."

There was some mumbling of surprise in the crowd. In the row behind me in the balcony, Mr. Ramponi stood up. "That not right. I no born here. I become citizen."

Judge Dickens pounded his gavel. "Sit down, Mr. Ramponi. This is not a town meeting."

Uncle Tomo tried to explain. "I come from another country. Just like men who started America."

"You dare to compare yourself to the patriots who fought and died for this country?" The DA lurched toward the witness box. "Especially after what your people pulled at Pearl Harbor!"

"Mr. Lashley—" The judge tried to slow him down, but Minnie's dad was blowing smoke like a runaway train.

"You have no loyalty to this country. You'd sell us out for thirty pieces of silver and a bowl of rice," Mr. Lashley said, shaking his finger at Uncle Tomo. "And that's exactly what you did when you killed Mr. Peck and blew up the factory, isn't it? Isn't it!"

"Mr. Lashley, that's enough!" Judge Dickens said.

Mr. Lashley moved to the jury box. "Mr. Fu-jita. Just answer one simple question. Do you want the United States to win this war? Do you want the United States to defeat Japan?"

The courtroom fell silent. For a long time, Uncle Tomo

didn't say anything. At last he shook his head, like he knew it was the wrong answer but it was the only one he could give. "No," he said.

"And that's why you sabotaged our airplane factory, isn't it!" barked the DA, inciting the crowd.

Judge Dickens pounded his gavel some more, but the crowd had already started to taunt and jeer Uncle Tomo: "Traitor!" "Murderer!"

"Order. Order!" said the judge.

Uncle Tomo seemed heartbroken. For a moment I thought he might even cry. But he didn't. He just looked at Kenji across the room and said, "War is wrong. For every country."

I had lucked out. They hadn't called me to the stand. Uncle Tomo's testimony had gone badly, but they hadn't shown one bit of proof that he'd killed Mr. Peck. As for the sabotage, the only witness was Farley, and you'd have to be a complete dope to believe anything he said. Everything was gonna be all right. Dad was coming home in a few days and he'd straighten it all out.

I waited for Kenji outside the courthouse for twenty minutes, but he didn't come out. Instead, it was Mr. Wylie who excused himself from talking to the reporters and approached me and my mom.

"Mrs. McGill, I'm going to call Bird to the stand tomorrow."

"Why?" I protested. "I don't know anything."

"The boy, Kenji, believes you do," Mr. Wylie said.

"Is that really necessary, Mr. Wylie?" my mom asked.

"Probably not. But I'd be risking a mistrial if I didn't pursue every possibility, no matter how ridiculous. We all want this thing over and done with as quickly as possible. Best thing for the town. I just wanted you to be prepared. See you tomorrow."

Once he was gone, Mom got real serious. "Bird. That man Mr. Fujita is on trial for his life. If you know something, you have to tell the truth."

I didn't say anything.

That night, Mom let me go visit Kenji in his room at the police station. It was really just the spare jail cell, but he had decorated it with his movie posters and stuff, so I guess it wasn't so bad. The only other time I had ever been in the jail was in third grade, when we went on a field trip to the police station. That time, there was a man in the cell trying to sleep when we came in. He was curled up on the bench, facing the wall. It was like when you see the lions or monkeys at the zoo, and all the kids make animal sounds and toss peanuts to get them to react, but all the animals want to do is lie there and pretend they're not being stared at all day. The kids kept bugging the man in jail, asking questions like "Do they let you go to the bathroom?" and "Why are you in jail? Did you kill someone?" The man finally got fed up and said it was because he got too drunk on Saturday night and punched somebody who kept asking him stupid questions.

Kenji hadn't gotten drunk or punched anybody, but there he was, in jail. It might have been, like the deputy said, to protect him, but any way you looked at it, he was still stuck in a cage like some animal at the zoo.

"You have to tell them who you saw, Bird," Kenji said.

"*Shhh*," I said. I looked through the cell bars and saw Deputy Steyer lift his head from his desk. I motioned for Kenji to lower his voice so the deputy couldn't hear.

"You don't understand. I don't know who it is," I whispered.

"But you know it wasn't my uncle," he said.

"Yeah. But it's more complicated than that," I told him.

"Can't you tell your mom?" he asked.

I shook my head. "She never believes me."

"Bird, if you don't tell someone, they're going to send him to jail," Kenji said.

I wracked my brain for some kind of solution. Even if I testified about the man in black, since I didn't know who he was, there was no way to prove any of what I said. They might think I just made it up to help Kenji. And the man in black would know I squealed, and so he would have to kill my family. Any way you sliced it, I was still just an eleven-year-old girl who everyone thought was nuts.

"I keep thinking, if somebody really smart, like the Green Hornet, was in this situation, what would he do?" I said.

"He wouldn't leave his best friend Kato hanging out to dry," Kenji said.

My eyes wandered to one of the movie posters on the

wall. It showed Spencer Tracy as Father Flanagan in *Boys Town*. In the movie, Father Flanagan is a priest who is like a father to a bunch of troublemaking orphans who nobody else cares about. He looked so wise and knowing. All of a sudden it hit me. Maybe there *was* someone who would believe me.

It was dark by the time I tiptoed into the church. There was no one around. Even the war widows had finished their rosaries and gone home. Father Krauss was extinguishing the last of the altar candles when he spotted me in the aisle.

"Hello, Bird. I've been expecting you."

"You have?"

"It's about your testimony tomorrow, isn't it?" he said confidently.

I nodded. "How did you know, Father?"

"Oh, a good shepherd always knows his flock." He reached up to draw the heavy cloth blackout shades over the stained-glass windows. "Could you help me with these, Bird?"

He tugged on the blinds and the sleeve of his robe slid up his arm. As the church went dark, I noticed something strange on his right forearm. It was a bandage. And it was funny, because it was right about the same place where I had bitten the man in black. My hand began to tremble.

"Wh-what happened to your arm, Father?"

He quickly covered his bandage with his sleeve.

"Oh, it's nothing. Hooked myself fishing is all," he said. "Still trying to catch something besides turnips for Sister Marilyn." His voice echoed throughout the darkness of the church. "Would you prefer to talk in the confessional?"

He moved toward me, his strong hand grasping my arm.

"No," I said, trying to wriggle away.

"They say it's good for the soul."

"I . . . I just remembered," I said, fighting free from his grip. "I have to go do something." I stumbled over myself and when I stepped backwards, I fell down between two of the pews.

"Ow!" I leapt to my feet and tried to run. But my pant leg got caught on the wooden kneeler.

"You've hurt yourself. Let me look at it," Father Krauss said.

"No! No, thanks." I yanked at my leg.

"Bird." He leaned down toward me, his black robe blocking out the light.

My pant leg tore loose, and I took off as fast as I could out the church door.

CHAPTER 14

The next day I nervously entered the courthouse with my mom. The crowds had grown so big that we were all mashed together like spawning salmon squeezing our way to the courtroom. For a moment, as we weaved through, I lost hold of Mom's hand. Suddenly, I felt someone shove me in the back, knocking me to the floor. It was Farley Peck, and within seconds he was on top of me with his forearm jammed in my back.

"If you got any birdbrained ideas about c-c-covering for that Jap kid's uncle," he whispered in my ear, "remember fires can start anyplace, anytime."

"Bird." Mom was there. She knelt down and helped me up.

"She fell," Farley said, pretending to help dust off my sleeve.

I pulled my arm away from him. "I think I need to use the bathroom," I told Mom.

"Okay," she said.

Farley glared at me as we walked away.

Just as I escaped into the bathroom, I saw Mrs. Lashley, Minnie's big-haired mom, corner my mom.

After splashing some cold water on my face, I shut off the faucet and checked my hair in the mirror. Through the air vent slats in the ladies' room door, I could hear my mom and Mrs. Lashley talking.

"Are you all right?" Mrs. Lashley whined. "I heard about that business at your house the other night."

"We're okay," said Mom.

"Children. They can be so foolish and reckless sometimes."

"Yes. I suppose so," Mom said.

"The Japanese boy seemed harmless enough at first. I suppose she didn't know better, but then, she's always been difficult. A bit of an oddball, wouldn't you say? I mean, a cute girl like her wanting to be called Bird. God bless you, you must have the patience of a saint."

I was getting ready to leave the ladies' room when I heard something crinkle as it slid under the door. I spun around to see a folded, lined piece of paper. It was some kind of note. I picked it up and opened it slowly.

> Are you clever enough to
> keep our secret?
> I'll be watching.

In an instant, I burst out the ladies' room door and ran smack into the mobs of people who were jamming the courthouse. I searched every face for the eyes, those dark, empty shark eyes.

Suddenly a hand grabbed my shoulder.

"Ahhh!" I screamed.

"Are you all right?" Father Krauss said. "You seemed a little strange last night."

I remembered his bandaged arm and tried not to scream again. Then I spotted my mom with Mrs. Lashley. I broke free and ran to her across the room.

Mrs. Lashley was still talking. "I know you'll make sure she does the right thing today and exposes that shifty-eyed Mr. Fujita. It will really go a long way toward salvaging her character."

"Character?" Suddenly Mom blew her top worse than the time I made a slingshot out of her stocking. She poked her finger at Mrs. Lashley. "That little girl of mine has more character in her little pinky than you and a whole army of those squirrel-faced Shirley Temple cutouts you and your cronies call daughters!"

150

"I beg your pardon!" Mrs. Lashley backed away from Mom and tripped on her high heels. When she plopped down on the floor, her hat fell off and her hair sort of spun around.

"And if I ever hear you talk about Bird like that again, so help me, Irene, I'll mop the floor with you and that woolly wig you keep on your head."

Mrs. Lashley clutched her hair—and it fell right off! I had always thought her hair looked funny, but I never guessed it wasn't attached to her head. Everyone in the small crowd that had gathered to watch burst out laughing. Mrs. Lashley tried to cover the bare patches on her balding head, but it was no use, so she raced into the bathroom in tears.

Mom grabbed my hand. "Come on."

The crowd parted for us and we marched straight toward the courtroom. It was like that scene in the movie *The Wizard of Oz* when all the Munchkins stand back to let Dorothy follow the yellow brick road. And all at once, maybe for the first time, I got the incredible feeling that this woman, who it seemed could only scold me or complain about having to clean up after me all the time, this woman who'd just cut Mrs. Lashley down about two sizes, this same woman was *my mom*, and I wanted everyone in town to know it.

It was finally my turn to be called. A minute later I was on the stand, trying hard not to fidget, but I couldn't help it. My eyes kept darting over all the people in the courtroom

151

who were watching me like I was a lightning bug in a jar. I wished I could just stare at the floor, but I could feel the eyes of Father Krauss on me, and it was like my eyes needed to run away until they found something safe to stare at.

Mr. Wylie finally grabbed my attention. "Don't be nervous, honey. All you need to do is tell the truth."

I nodded, and took a sip of water.

"Now, on the night of the explosion, you and Kenji were in the woods by Geneseo Bay, trying to take a picture, is that correct?"

"Y-yes."

The crowd chuckled a little.

"Did you see the defendant, Mr. Fujita, coming back through the woods after the explosion, like Farley testified?"

I shook my head. "No, sir."

"Did you see Farley Peck that night?"

"No." I'd seen Mr. Peck under Father Krauss's boat. Of course, if I mentioned that, everyone would wonder why I hadn't said anything about it until now. They'd probably think I was making the whole thing up just to help my friend. Maybe they'd even think *I* was the one who killed Mr. Peck.

"Now, I want you to think back. Think back, real hard. Did you see anyone in the woods that night? The *real* person responsible for the murder of Mr. Peck and the sabotage at the Warhawk engine plant, perhaps?"

Mr. Lashley leapt to his feet. "Real person? Objection, Your Honor."

"Overruled," said the judge. "She can answer."

I could answer? Not without ruining either my life or Kenji's.

"Um . . . ," I mumbled. I tried to imagine that Dad was there. What would he have done? What would he have said? Something really smart, I bet. I looked around the courtroom. Kenji's eyes were pleading with me to tell everyone about the man in black. Then I saw Farley sneering in the front row. He reached into his pocket and pulled out his dad's Zippo lighter. He flipped it open and playfully flicked the wheel, trying to threaten me. I was sure he would have loved to see me open my big mouth so that the man in black could shut me up for good. Deputy Steyer cocked his jaw, wondering what I was going to say.

"Could you repeat the question?" I said, stalling for time.

Mr. Wylie cleared his throat and gave me a big-eyed look like I was a three-year-old or something. "I'll make it easier for you, honey. Do you know who killed Mr. Peck?"

I looked down at the crumpled threat in my hand. *I'll be watching.*

When I looked up, my eyes got caught by Father Krauss's. He gave the tiniest smile, which shivered the hair on my neck and forearms. If he really was the man in black, why didn't he just kill me the other night? Why risk me talking in court? Was it because he knew no one would believe me? Or was it that if he did kill me or my family, then

153

everyone would know it wasn't Uncle Tomo who killed Mr. Peck and bombed the factory? Maybe that was it. He needed me alive. He wanted me to testify. He knew that if I agreed with Kenji, it would make Kenji and Uncle Tomo seem as crazy as everyone in town already thought *I* was. Maybe Uncle Tomo would be better off if I just kept my mouth shut? I looked away and spotted Mom nodding for me to go ahead and answer. It was like the whole world was waiting to hear what I had to say.

"Do you know who killed Mr. Peck?" Mr. Wylie repeated.

"No," I said. It was sort of the truth. I didn't know for sure. At least, that was what I told myself.

The spectators in the courtroom let out one big sigh, as if I had just poked a hole in their big birthday balloon or something. Some of them began to grumble among themselves. Kenji looked hurt and mad, like I had just punched him in the nose. Farley flashed his crooked grin and flicked his dad's lighter closed.

"Mr. Lashley?" The judge broke the silence of the room.

"The prosecution rests, Your Honor," Mr. Lashley said.

The judge turned to me. "You may step down."

I lowered my eyes and slunk past Kenji and Uncle Tomo.

Less than fifteen minutes later, the jury was filing back into the courtroom with their decision. I couldn't tell if that was a good sign or a bad one. When Mom won "Best Tomato" at the county fair, the judges took two hours to decide. But in second grade when Minnie sat down on chewing gum on her seat, the teacher didn't even ask Farley's side of things before giving him a week of blackboard duty right on the spot. I guessed a quick decision meant everyone on the jury pretty much agreed from the start. Whether they agreed that Uncle Tomo didn't kill Mr. Peck or sabotage the plane factory was what we'd find out in a minute.

The room got quieter than it had been all week. It felt like everyone was holding their breath.

Finally the judge asked, "Members of the jury, have you reached a verdict?"

The elderly man in the first seat of the jury box answered, "We have, Your Honor."

"Mr. Foreman?"

The elderly man stood up. He cleared his throat. "For the charges of sabotage, espionage, and murder in the first degree, we the jury find the defendant . . . guilty on all counts."

What? I couldn't believe it. It had to be a mistake.

"No!" Kenji screamed. "He didn't do anything."

Judge Dickens pounded his gavel for quiet, but Farley laughed and cheered right along with most of the spectators.

Uncle Tomo looked devastated. The guards started to handcuff him and he dropped his head to his chest like he was ashamed—even though he knew he was innocent. And I felt like I did in second grade, when I kept my mouth shut and didn't admit that it was *me*, not Farley, who put that gum on Minnie's chair, and instead I let Farley take the blame since he was probably guilty of something else anyway. Some "American" I turned out to be. I felt about as worthless as a three-dollar bill.

"Order. Order," the judge demanded. "The court will schedule sentencing for next week. Jury is dismissed." The crowd resumed its chatter and I heard Judge Dickens say to himself, "May God forgive us."

I rushed over to Kenji. "It'll be okay. My dad will straighten everything out when he comes home, I promise."

Kenji turned away in all the commotion and was quickly escorted out of the courtroom by Deputy Steyer.

I managed to squeeze my way to Agent Barson and tugged on his sleeve. "What's gonna happen to Kenji?"

"He has no other family. I'm afraid he'll have to join his parents in the internment camp."

"Why?" I said. "He didn't do anything."

"I'm sorry" was all Agent Barson said.

The streetlight outside the police station made my shadow look six feet tall on the sidewalk. But I felt about six inches tall. I was no expert on friendship, but I would have bet that standing by and letting Kenji get shipped across the country to an internment camp put me in the running for the "Worst Friend of the Year" award.

A soft summer rain was just starting to fall as I stood at the door, pleading with the deputy to let me in.

"But Deputy Steyer, I have to talk to him."

"He said he doesn't want to see you, Bird."

"I can explain everything," I said.

"There's nothing I can do," the deputy said.

"But I'm his friend."

Suddenly, a sniffling voice from the other room yelled out, "I don't have any friends!"

The deputy shooed me out. "I'm sorry, Bird. It's late. You'll have to go."

I started to leave, then stopped. I talked loud enough so I knew Kenji could hear. "Deputy? If he asks, tell him it's *Belinda*."

The deputy rubbed his chin, confused.

"That's my real name," I said. "If he still cares to know."

"Belinda," the deputy repeated. "I'll tell him."

"Thanks."

As I turned around, I heard a sound. It was music. Kenji was playing the jitterbug record that he and I had danced to. Suddenly, the needle shrieked, and there was a smash—like someone shattering a record into a hundred pieces on the arm of a chair.

I lowered my head in the rain and decided to take the long way home.

Back at home, I sat staring at the radio as it played some stupid, happy swing music. Mom had almost finished mending my dress that had been damaged in the flour-bombing incident.

"You did everything you could," she said to me.

"No I didn't. Dad would've done more."

"It's not your fault, Bird," she said.

But I knew that wasn't true. The whole thing was my fault.

I was changing the station to hear if there was any news of the war, when the doorbell rang. Margaret leapt up and checked through the blinds.

"It's for me," she said, fluffing her hair.

All I could think was, *Poor Lieutenant Peppel. That was my fault, too.*

I heard her run and open the door, all a-giggle. "Hello, Vernon."

"Hi. Is Mrs. McGill home?"

There was something about the way he said "McGill" that made all the muscles in my stomach twist.

"Yeah," Margaret said. "Mom?"

I got up and followed Mom as she walked to the door, wiping her hands on her apron.

Lieutenant Peppel was standing in the rain with his eyes to the ground. He removed his hat. "Mrs. McGill. I was asked to deliver this on account of we've become somewhat acquainted and . . ."

His voice cracked and I got the sense that he was fighting to keep from shaking.

"Here." He slowly held out a brown military envelope.

Mom took it from him uneasily. It was a telegram. She

couldn't bring herself to open it. "What happened, Lieutenant?" She handed it back to him. "What does it say?"

He swallowed hard, like Dad did that time he had to tell me my kitty got run over. "Ma'am . . . your husband's plane was lost during naval landing maneuvers."

"What?" said Margaret. "What are you talking about?"

"Your father was testing a new fighter. His plane crashed in the ocean. He was killed."

I kept waiting for Lieutenant Peppel to start laughing and admit this was all a joke. It was a really awful joke, and I wished he would hurry up and start laughing. But all he did was hold that ugly brown envelope.

Then Mom turned to Margaret and said, "Take Alvin and Bird upstairs."

Margaret got all pale and grabbed my arm, but I ripped it free.

"No!" I clutched Mom's leg and I wasn't letting go for anything. Margaret gave up and carried Alvin upstairs.

Mom looked at the envelope in the lieutenant's hand. "Open it for me, please."

Lieutenant Peppel opened it. He reached in and slowly pulled out Dad's bent and burnt dog tags. I knew they were his because Dad's wedding ring was still dangling from the chain. That was when Mom started to shake, and shudder, and sob.

I flew at the lieutenant, pounding my fists on him. "You're lying! I don't believe you!"

He just stood there and let me hit him.

"It's a lie! Dad's okay. I know he is," I cried.

Finally, Mom pulled me away.

"No, no, no!" I echoed over and over until my crying felt like it was coming from somewhere outside me. I buried my tears deep in the folds of Mom's faded dress, waiting and hoping to somehow wake up from this awful nightmare.

CHAPTER

15

I never used to think rain had any color, but looking up on the day of Dad's funeral, I could see I was wrong. It was definitely a gray rain falling from the sky onto the empty casket in the Geneseo cemetery. It was the dirtiest, ugliest gray I had ever seen. There was a military color guard firing rifle shots into the sky, but I couldn't even hear them. It was the same sort of numb feeling I got when I went flying and my ears wanted to pop but they wouldn't. Only now I felt that way all over. Like I was filling with air and about to burst.

Lieutenant Peppel had his arm around Margaret like it

was pretty much the only thing holding her up. Mom gripped Alvin's hand and mine and looked straight ahead, standing like a rock, pretending she was tough. But when she looked me in the eyes, all that toughness turned to Jell-O and she broke down.

Then, so did I.

From behind me I felt a soft, gloved hand on my shoulder. It was the Widow Gorman. She stepped forward and offered me her handkerchief. She was crying, too, but there was a strength in her face that I had never seen before. She squeezed my shoulder and it was then that I realized that the tears rolling down her wrinkled cheeks were just like mine. And they hurt just as much to let out. We clutched each other's hand and held on tight. There was nothing else we could do.

It was late afternoon before I felt like eating much of anything. Now I understood why Widow Gorman got so skinny after her son died. When I walked into our kitchen, I found Margaret trying to get Alvin to eat some potato salad while Mom slowly mounted a stepladder to replace the faded blue star in our window with a shiny new gold one.

The sight of that gold star was too much. It sent me bursting out the back door into the rain.

I furiously hauled myself up to the roof of our barn and planted myself there. There was a P-40 squadron flying formation in the distance. It didn't matter. Without Dad, I knew I would never fly a P-40 Warhawk. Maybe I would just stay up there on the roof forever.

A few minutes later the ladder creaked and Mom carefully climbed onto the roof. I didn't think she'd ever been up there before. She didn't say anything, just sat on the wet shingles next to me, watching the P-40s. After a little while, the planes flew off, disappearing into the clouds, and the only sound left was the rain *pat-pat-pat*ting on the roof.

"When I was your age, my father took me into Providence to buy a black dress." She tried to smile. But I couldn't bring myself to smile back. "And want to know something funny?" she asked.

I didn't say anything.

"I was just like you, Bird. I didn't like to wear dresses, either. But this was for the funeral of my favorite aunt, Belinda, so I put one on. She was a spinster. That means she never married, and when she died, they said she died alone. My father said it was because the world had no place for a woman on her own. It was probably true, but I didn't like the sound of it. All the same, it was always in the back of my mind, anytime I got the urge to do something girls weren't *supposed* to do." Mom turned to look at me. "But *your* daddy wasn't like mine. He let you do all the things that I'd wanted to do when I was a girl. Sometimes, I think maybe I was jealous of that."

"I can't do it, Mom. I can't fly without him."

"Maybe you don't have to. Maybe you can take him with you. Here." She touched my heart. "Inside."

"Hmmph. You don't believe stuff like that . . . do you?"

Mom looked up at the gray sky. "I'd like to," she said.

I didn't tell her, but part of me would have liked to believe it, too.

Then Mom surprised me. "You know, I believe you really did see a submarine, or something in the bay," she said.

"You do?" I said.

"Um-hmm." She wrapped her arm around my shoulder. Tight. "I think we're gonna need to believe in a lot of things to get through this."

"But it hurts, Mom," I said, and I started to cry again.

"I know." She pulled me close. "It hurts me, too."

Later that night, we were all huddled under the covers on Mom and Dad's big, warm bed while the rain pelted the window outside. My head was cradled on one of Mom's strong arms. Alvin and Margaret were embraced by the other.

"Will you tell us something?" I asked quietly. "About Dad."

Mom thought for a moment. Then she started to laugh. "Well, when he was younger, your father wanted to be . . . a famous tap dancer."

"Dad?" I hadn't even thought my dad could dance.

"When we met, I was an aspiring showgirl and your dad promised me we were going to take Broadway by storm."

Just the way she said it, Mom seemed years younger.

"I never knew that," Margaret said, looking kind of impressed.

"You know," Mom said, "we had a lot of dreams, your dad and I."

"But not anymore," I added.

"Oh no, Bird. I still have dreams. And you all must have them, too." She looked at us and tried to keep from crying. "He'd want that, you know."

It sounded weird, the way she was talking about him, like she knew he was gone but he was still sort of there, with us. But at the same time it felt totally right. Maybe that was what made it so hard to believe he was really dead, because nothing felt changed in my heart. I could still talk to him, and when I closed my eyes, I still felt him watching me, like a copilot sitting next to me, flying right seat.

"Promise me?" she said. "Promise us both that you'll still have dreams."

"I promise, Mom," said Margaret.

Little Alvin followed. "Cross my heart."

In my pocket, my hand reached down and felt the crumpled note from the man in black. Dad had been right. A friend had found me. Kenji. Just like Dad had said. Only I'd let him down. Betrayed him. All because I was scared. Of what? Something bad happening? It already had. Fear was always getting in the way, always stopping you from doing the really great stuff, the real important stuff. I was sick of it. What was it Dad had told me? The only one I needed to believe in me was me. For the first time since before Dad left, I knew exactly what I needed to do.

"I promise," I said.

The next morning, before the sun came up and before anyone else was awake, I quietly slipped downstairs and out our front door.

I reached Deputy Steyer's house in the predawn darkness and checked to see if anyone was watching before I knocked, softly.

"Deputy Steyer?" I knocked again. "Deputy Steyer?"

I was walking around the side of his house, looking for his bedroom window, when I spotted a light on in the basement. I remember wondering what he was doing up that early. I knelt down and peered through the muddy window.

At a lighted bench, Deputy Steyer was working, hunched over something, some kind of box, while the radio played loudly in the background. Then I realized what it was he was working on. It was Kenji's phonograph. He must have been fixing it up before Kenji's train ride to Manzanar. I thought that was kind of nice.

The radio announcer was reporting something about "our boys" being "on heightened alert" after the sinking of some supply boat off North Carolina, and about how President

166

Roosevelt planned to cut short his whistle-stop tour, or something like that.

That was when Deputy Steyer stopped all of a sudden and turned up the volume. Then I heard:

"President Roosevelt will be making his final stop in Providence, Rhode Island, later this morning."

I tapped on the window and the deputy jumped about a foot and spun around with a hunting knife in his hand. Then he saw that it was just me.

"Bird! What are you doing here?" He shoved the knife under some papers on the workbench.

"I didn't mean to scare you," I hollered. "Can I come in?"

He quickly closed up Kenji's phonograph and motioned to me to meet him at the front door.

I walked back around to the front, but he only opened the door a crack. "Look," he said, "I'm sorry about having to send your friend away, but—"

"I know who killed Mr. Peck," I blurted out.

The deputy looked around, sort of worried-like, and said, "Maybe you'd better come inside."

Deputy Steyer led me into his house. I had never been in there before. It was darker than I had expected. And the walls were missing something, but at first I wasn't exactly sure what. Then I realized what it was. The deputy didn't have any pictures of his family or friends anywhere.

He took me into the kitchen, where a pot of coffee was percolating.

"Now, what's this all about, Bird?" he asked.

I dug into my pocket and handed him the crumpled note. "The killer sent me that before I testified."

He read it silently. His eyes narrowed. Then he set it down.

"He knows I can identify him," I said.

Deputy Steyer turned away from me to grab his pot of coffee. "*Who* knows?"

"The spy," I told him.

The deputy jerked back toward me so fast, he accidentally splashed hot coffee on his arm and uttered some word under his breath. I thought I must have been really tired, because it sounded like the same word the killer had said, *Scheisse.*

"Oh my gosh! Are you okay?" I asked him.

"It's all right," he said, calm again. His arm had to hurt pretty bad, because it was already turning red and swelling a little where the coffee had scalded him, but he seemed to completely ignore it somehow.

"Boy, you're a lot tougher than I am." I grabbed the nearby butter dish. "Here, let me put some of this on it. My mother always said—" But as I pulled back his sleeve to rub the butter on his burn, I saw *it* and froze.

It was a small bite mark, right there on his forearm. It was about the size of my mouth.

He quickly yanked down his sleeve to cover the mark. Slowly, I began to back away from him.

"What's the matter, Bird?" he asked calmly.

"N-n-nothing. I just remembered. I was supposed to call m-m-my mother," I stuttered like Farley.

He carefully latched the kitchen door behind his back.

"I don't think that's going to be possible, *Liebchen*." Suddenly his eyes got this crazy gloss, like Wendy's dog Sparky looked when he got rabies. He lunged for me, but I grabbed his coffee cup and splashed the scalding liquid right in his face.

"Ahhh!" he shrieked in pain.

I rushed past him and fought to unlock the kitchen door with my shaking hands. But there was a strange double bolt, and I couldn't figure out how to unlatch it.

"Help! Help!" I screamed, pounding and rattling the door.

The deputy recovered and snatched my ankle. I fell to the floor, bumping my head, and in a flash it was like I was trapped in a tunnel with my only focus reaching the light at the other end. My mind was all blurry shapes and sounds, with a million voices telling every muscle and nerve in my body to escape somehow, now! I managed to kick my leg free and I ran for the other doorway, which led down to the basement.

But Deputy Steyer was right behind me. With all my might, I slammed the basement door behind me, right on his fingers.

"Ow!" he cried out.

I tried to shut the door all the way, but he was too

strong. He threw it open, knocking me off balance and sending me tumbling, backwards, down the hard wooden stairs.

I rolled to a stop somewhere on the basement floor. I tried to get up, but my head was ringing and my vision was blurred. My ribs ached and it hurt like heck to breathe. I looked up and saw the deputy's shadowy form at the top of the stairs. The deputy wiped the coffee off his face, took a moment to fix his mussed-up hair, then methodically marched down the stairs toward me. All the while, I could see a twisted smile growing across his face.

"I was right," I said. "About the sub, and the spies. Everything."

"Yes, Bird. I'm the only one who's believed you all along," he said, laughing. "Too bad I'm the only one who ever will."

I couldn't get up. I couldn't move a muscle. It felt like I had been turned into stone. I realized then I wasn't going to be able to run away. There was no way out. This was the end.

That was when I started to think about dying. I wondered how Mr. Peck must have felt. Did Dad have time to think about dying? I was too terrified to even scream. Probably nobody could hear me anyway. But my mind was still thinking a million thoughts at once. *I wish I had never seen the Genny in the bay. . . . I should have spoken up in second grade and said it was me, not Farley, who stuck the gum on Minnie's chair. . . . I wish I could tell Mom how much I love her. . . . I wonder if I'll see Dad and Grandpa McGill. . . . Are there air-planes in Heaven? I hope Kenji knows I'm sorry. . . .*

The deputy took off his belt and wrapped it around his fists like he was getting ready to strangle someone. Then he knelt down over me.

I closed my eyes and made a wish that this was all somehow just a bad dream.

BAM, BAM, BAM.

I opened my eyes. Someone or something was pounding on Deputy Steyer's front door. In my hazy state of mind, I heard a familiar voice call from outside:

"Deputy Steyer? It's Agent Barson. I'm dropping off the boy."

The deputy stood. He carefully unwrapped the belt from his fists.

"Just a minute," he answered, so calm and cool you would've never guessed that he'd just been trying to kill an eleven-year-old girl. He stuffed an oily rag in my mouth, knotted it around my head, and tied my hands behind my back with some rope.

Agent Barson called out, "Sorry I'm so early, but my boss needs to use this car to be in Providence for President Roosevelt's arrival."

Deputy Steyer stepped over me and walked to his workbench. He carefully carried Kenji's phonograph upstairs. I heard a clank as he bolted the basement door. Then the front door was opened, and through the basement window I caught bits of the conversation outside.

"Good morning," Deputy Steyer said.

"What happened?" asked Agent Barson.

There was a pause. The deputy didn't answer.

"Spill some coffee?"

"Oh, that. Yes," the deputy said, laughing.

I was finally able to work myself up to my feet. I couldn't free my hands. I tried to climb the stairs, but with my hands tied and my head still spinning from my earlier fall, I lost my balance and wound up tumbling back to the basement floor.

Then everything went black.

By the time I came to, it was too late. I bellied onto Deputy Steyer's workbench under the basement window and stood up on my feet, but I was still too short to reach the window. All I could do was listen as Agent Barson's car and then the deputy's car pulled away.

I tried to wriggle my hands free, but the rope was too tight. On top of that, the oily gag in my mouth tasted horrible. I shook my head and twisted my neck to try and loosen it, but it was no use. I tried to squat down to climb off the workbench but lost my balance and fell right on my butt.

"Ow!" I'd landed on something hard, under some papers. I reached my hand back to remove the lumpy object. I felt around under the papers and then, "Dang it!" I cut my hand.

It was a knife! It must've been the one Deputy Steyer had shoved under the papers when he saw me looking through the window. I felt around and grabbed it again, carefully this time. I slid the blade between my wrists and began sawing at the rope.

Once my hands were free I untied the dirty rag around my mouth. Yuk. I tried to spit out the oily taste. As I massaged the rope burns on my wrist, something about the knife caught my eye. The black wood-grained handle looked familiar. Two large letters, *F* and *P*, were crookedly carved into it. I had had that knife shoved in my face by Farley enough times to realize it was his. The same one he gave to his dad when we were spying on him that day in the woods. The deputy must have stolen it when he killed Farley's dad. I grabbed the knife, climbed down off the workbench, ran up the stairs, and tried to jimmy the basement door lock open.

It was no use. Deputy Steyer had dead-bolted the door. The only way out was to break the door down, and I wasn't strong enough to do that. There had to be another way out. I looked across the room, at the window.

I ran back down the stairs and climbed onto the workbench. But the window was still too high for me to reach. Maybe if I stood on the stool on top of the workbench? I climbed down and cleared the workbench. There were coils of wire, maps, newspaper clippings—all kinds of junk—on it. There was my P-40 manual! I stuffed it in my back pocket. There were also some strange jars of liquid that looked like the kind our science teacher would use, and a metal can of black powder with red writing on the side. I moved them off the bench top onto the floor, but I stopped as I was about to set down the powder can. I'd seen something like it before. It was at the trial, when Agent Barson was saying all that boring stuff about chemistry and ingredients to make explosives. This was the same kind of can as the one they'd found in Uncle Tomo's apartment. The one Uncle Tomo said he'd never seen before. Deputy Steyer had put it there. He set off the bomb in the P-40 factory and then made it look like Uncle Tomo did it. And that got me thinking: What the heck was the deputy doing to Kenji's phonograph?

Of course! Deputy Steyer had been making another bomb. But why put a bomb in a kid's record player? I had no idea, but I had to get out and warn Kenji. I wrapped the knife in some newspaper clippings so it wouldn't cut me, and I put it in my other back pocket.

I lifted the stool onto the workbench. It was metal, and heavier than I thought it was gonna be. The seat swiveled around, making it hard to stand on. I climbed up and knelt on top of it. Then I got up onto my feet. But one leg of the stool was shorter than the others, and the stool teetered. The seat spun around and I felt myself falling. I grabbed on to the ledge of the window and had to use my legs to balance the stool back upright. I reached back and got the knife out of my pocket. I covered my face with my arm, and *CRASH!* I smashed the basement window with the knife butt. I cleared out as much of the busted glass as I could, then pulled myself up. Crawling through the jagged window frame, I scraped my arms and tore my pants, but I didn't care.

Once I was out, I raced down the street to the nearest house and pounded on the door with my fists. "Hello! Is anyone home? Hello?"

It seemed like forever, but at last the inside lights turned on and someone opened the door. It was Mrs. Simmons, still half asleep.

"Mrs. Simmons? Call the deputy! No, wait, don't call him. Call the FBI, or the Army or something. Deputy Steyer's gonna blow up my friend Kenji!"

"Uh-huh. Whatever you say, Bird." She promptly slammed her door to go back to bed.

"Mrs. Simmons. Mrs. Simmons!" But she wouldn't come back.

I ran for another house, across the street. This one was a dump. Out back there was a smelly chicken coop—and someone was inside.

"Hey! You in the chicken coop!" I hollered.

Two big feet, covered in putrid chicken crap, stepped out. It was Farley Peck.

"What the heck are you d-d-doing?" he said.

"Farley! You've gotta help me," I babbled. "Somebody just tried to kill me."

"Yeah? Good." He turned around to head back into the chicken coop.

"You don't understand. Deputy Steyer is the spy! He's the one who killed your father."

He looked back at me. "You're nuts." Then he started walking away.

"Wait!" I grabbed him by the sleeve. "I found this." I unwrapped the newspaper clippings I'd put around the knife. He instantly recognized the knife and snatched it out of my hand.

"Where d-d-did you get this?"

"I found it—"

But he choked me by the collar of my shirt before I could finish.

"Where?" he demanded.

"In Deputy Steyer's basement!"

He rolled the knife over in his hand. "My dad g-g-gave this to me when I was six." He touched it slowly, the same way I held my dad's dog tags. Then Farley, the big bad bully, started to sniffle. He turned away to wipe his nose on his sleeve.

"It's the deputy," I said. "It has been all along. He's the spy. Everyone wanted the killer to look like Kenji or Uncle Tomo. They never thought he might look just like us."

Farley clenched his fist under my chin. "If you're lying—"

"I'm not. Swear on my dad, I'm not."

He looked me in the eyes, and maybe it was because I looked so scared, or maybe it was because he just realized I had lost my dad, too, but for once he actually believed me.

"What do you need me to do?" he asked, with no stutter at all.

"I don't know." I tried to think for a moment. I happened

to glance down at the newspaper clippings in my hand. The ones I had wrapped the knife in. The ones from Deputy Steyer's workbench. One of them wasn't really a news clipping. It was just the weekly train schedule. The 8:00 a.m. arrival time for Providence was circled. Another one was from the front page of the *Geneseo Post* in March. The headline read: PRESIDENT ROOSEVELT TO STOP IN PROVIDENCE THIS SUMMER.

"Oh my God!"

"What?" Farley said.

"It's the President. That's who the deputy's really after. He put a bomb in Kenji's record player, and if we don't stop him, he's gonna use it to kill the President." I gave Farley the circled train schedule and the newspaper clipping about President Roosevelt. "Find Agent Barson. Show him these, and tell him everything." But Farley didn't move. That jerk! He just couldn't stand to help me or Kenji. Even if it meant saving the President!

I shook him. "What's the matter with you!?"

"It says here the President's train arrives at eight. It's at least seven-fifteen right now, Bird. The deputy's got too much of a head start for anyone to catch him by car. And the local train already left for Providence. There's no way to catch him."

He was right, of course. It was hopeless. I plopped down on the ground. Right onto the P-40 manual in my pocket. The manual that said—on page 13, section 3, if I remembered correctly—that the Curtiss P-40 Warhawk could reach a top speed of 362 miles an hour. Providence was about 180 miles away. At top speed, the Warhawk could get there in about thirty minutes.

I leapt back to my feet, looked around, and spied a rusty bicycle that was leaning against the chicken coop. I mounted it and told Farley, "Find Agent Barson."

"Where are you going?" he asked.

"To try and catch a plane."

CHAPTER 16

By the time I made it to my house, my legs were aching so much from pedaling Farley's rusty piece-of-junk bike, I felt like I'd been running through knee-deep pancake batter. I bet Farley never once oiled that darn bicycle chain. I flopped the bike against the barn and spotted Alvin playing in our backyard.

"Where's . . . Mom?" I asked, between gasps for air.

"Out looking for you."

"And Margaret?"

"They went looking for you, that way." He pointed

toward the pond at the back of our field, and I was off and running.

When I made it to the weeds near the pond, I found Lieutenant Peppel's motor scooter on its side, but no sign of Margaret or the lieutenant. I cut through the weeds and followed the sound of laughter and a trail of discarded outer clothes leading to the pond.

"Margaret?" I called out.

"Oh God! It's my little sister." I heard a splash, like someone diving underwater, just as I burst into the open to find Margaret swimming in her underwear.

"Margaret! I need your help," I called out.

"Where the heck have you been, Bird?" she said, trying to hide the fact that she was standing in our pond—in her *bra*! "Um. We've been, I mean *I've* been looking all over for you."

"Tell Lieutenant Peppel we need his P-40!"

"Lieutenant Peppel? He's not here."

"It's important, Margaret!"

Something swirled under the water next to her.

Some bubbles came up, the water thrashed, and finally, the lieutenant couldn't hold his breath any longer and popped up for air. "Sorry, Margaret."

"Lieutenant! Deputy Steyer is going to blow up the President!" I yelled. "We have to beat him to the train station!"

He rolled his eyes. "Kid, I tell you what. I promise, I'll take you flying tomorrow."

I saw I was getting nowhere fast, and there wasn't a lot of time to convince him. Then I spotted his uniform. A pilot's uniform.

"Thanks!" I snatched it up and was on the run again.

"Hey!" the lieutenant hollered to Margaret. "She's taking my clothes!"

"Bird!" Margaret screamed after me.

But I had a pretty good head start. By the time they'd splashed their way ashore, I was already bouncing through the field on Lieutenant Peppel's motor scooter.

I hadn't stopped to think that I'd never ridden a motor scooter before, and since my legs didn't quite reach the running boards, it was even harder to balance. So every time I started to swerve and fall, I ended up cranking the throttle on the handlebar to compensate. This kept me from wiping out, but my lack of balance combined with the burst of power every time I used the throttle left me swerving left and right like I did when I first learned to ride a bike.

As I approached the gate outside the airfield, I could see that the sentry was already looking suspiciously at the wiggly trajectory I was taking, not to mention my wildly oversized uniform and helmet. This was never gonna work. I acted like I was slowing down.

"Hold your horses there, Lindbergh." The sentry held out his hand.

I hit the gas and tried to swerve around, but instead headed straight for him. He had to dive into the mud to

181

avoid getting hit. Then he scrambled into the guard shack and hit the siren.

I nearly wiped out as the scooter tires got caught in the deep muddy truck grooves that had been cut into the field after the recent rains, but I regained my balance and raced toward the hangar. Looking back over my shoulder, I saw that a military police jeep was already speeding onto the tarmac and heading toward the guard shack.

Moments later, I dumped the scooter against the hangar wall by Lieutenant Peppel's P-40. The uniform obviously wasn't gonna work as a disguise, so I tossed it aside and clambered up the wing into the cockpit. Just as I did, I spotted Lieutenant Peppel pedaling Farley's rusty bicycle. He was wearing the only thing he must have been able to find—Margaret's summer dress! He knew exactly where I was headed, so he blew past the sentry and took off toward me in the hangar.

I settled into the P-40 cockpit, switched on the magneto, and the starter began to spin up and whine. The twelve cylinders fired over and the stacks coughed that lovely smell of airplane exhaust. It wasn't until I stretched out my feet to test the rudder pedals that I realized something was wrong. My feet didn't feel anything. I looked down and saw that my legs were about six inches too short.

When I looked up, Lieutenant Peppel had already pulled on his uniform and was scrambling onto the wing. I quickly hand-cranked the cockpit canopy the rest of the way shut, just before he could reach in and grab me. He pounded the glass.

"Bird! You've got to stop," he commanded.

I shook my head. "Deputy Steyer's going to kill the President! He already tried to kill me." I must have looked pretty scared, because the stern look on his face kind of melted away. I crossed my heart. "Honest," I said.

That was when he noticed the rope burns on my wrists. And the bruise on my forehead. "Did he do that to you?"

I nodded.

Then Lieutenant Peppel got a really angry look on his face. "Open the cockpit. I'm coming with you."

I cranked back the canopy and he climbed in behind me.

"You really believe me?" I asked.

"I reckon I do," he said with a smile.

Meanwhile, the M.P. jeep was heading straight toward us.

"If we stop now, we won't get there in time to save the President," I told him.

"Okay," he said.

I checked our clearance, just like Dad had taught me, and Lieutenant Peppel taxied us out of the hangar, full speed ahead. I wasn't really sure what the heck we were gonna do, but my heart was pumping way too fast for me to stop and think about it. Lieutenant Peppel pushed my feet out of his way so he could control the rudder pedals, and the big shark mouth roared out toward the runway.

The P-40 had such a big nose that you couldn't see

anything in front of you, whether you were eleven or one hundred eleven. The only way to see the ground was to swerve left and right, in a zigzag. As we zigzagged, the M.P. jeep pulled up alongside. It was Captain Winston, riding with the M.P.'s. And they all had their guns drawn.

"Lieutenant! Stop that plane this instant!" Captain Winston ordered.

"Can't, sir. It's a matter of life and death!"

"Then I'm coming aboard!" Captain Winston shouted to his men, "Move me close to the wing!"

The captain chose his moment and leapt onto the mighty Warhawk wing. The lieutenant ruddered hard right to try and shake him off. Captain Winston slid to the edge and rolled right off the wingtip.

The lieutenant shook his head woefully. "I'm gonna be court-martialed for sure."

Behind us on the tarmac, the jeep skidded to a stop and the M.P.'s got out to make sure Captain Winston was all right.

As we taxied past the control tower to line up for takeoff, I could see the traffic controllers sticking their heads out the windows of the tower and pointing at us frantically. I heard someone shout over my helmet intercom: "Who or what is flying that plane?"

The lieutenant hollered to me over the engine, "Now can you tell me where we're going?"

"The train station. In Providence," I said.

I pulled on my goggles. Lieutenant Peppel shoved the

throttle full-forward and we accelerated like a stone from a slingshot.

Suddenly I was aware of yelling and the roar of an engine. Only it wasn't our engine. I poked my head out the side of the cockpit and oil splattered all over my goggles. I quickly wiped them clean and screamed, "Watch out, Lieutenant!"

Dead ahead of us, a T-6 trainer, a tank of an airplane, had just landed on the opposite end of the runway, blocking our escape.

"Dad-gum pilot trainee, he landed on the wrong end of the runway!"

I checked the instruments. "We've already built up too much speed to stop!"

"I don't know if there's enough runway to clear it!" Lieutenant Peppel screamed back.

"Well, we can't turn around." I pointed to our rear.

Lieutenant Peppel poked his head out, looking backwards. "It's Captain Winston again. And he's gaining on us." But when the lieutenant turned to face forward again, our Allison V-12 engine coughed a big spurt of juicy exhaust and Lieutenant Peppel was suddenly blinded by oil and gas.

"Aieeehhh!" he screamed in pain. He dropped the control stick and I instinctively grabbed it, fighting to hold us steady.

"I've got it!" I told him.

"Pull up, pull up!" he cried.

Directly ahead, the big barrel nose of the oncoming T-6 was only thirty yards away and closing. I shut my eyes and summoned all the guts I could. With all my strength, I pulled the stick to my belly.

The mighty Warhawk fighter nose lifted off the ground, clearing the oncoming T-6 by inches, and we tore into the air like a screaming hurricane.

"I did it, I did it!" I rejoiced.

But before Lieutenant Peppel could crank our canopy shut, the gusting wind blew my P-40 manual right out of the cockpit.

"My pilot's manual!"

Lieutenant Peppel rubbed his eyes. "I can't see, Peach-pit." He gritted his teeth. "Looks like we're both gonna have to fly her."

With a lump in my throat I answered, "I hope one of us can remember how to land this thing."

CHAPTER 17

From the outside, the P-40 might have seemed to be flying pretty smoothly, skipping over the clouds as we traced the highway north.

But inside the cockpit was another story. Nothing in that manual could have prepared me for flying the real thing. My whole body was as taut as a tightrope as I white-knuckled the stick while the oil-blinded Lieutenant Peppel worked the rudder and guided my hands on the controls.

"Ease up a little," he told me. "Take a breath. Dip your wings."

I took a breath like he said. Then I tipped left and scanned the road below for the deputy's car.

"Any sign of 'em?" the lieutenant asked.

"Negative," I answered.

"We need to get the captain on the radio," he yelled.

I adjusted the transmitter like he told me, and we eventually locked on to the crackly voice from the tower.

"Okay, here's the lieutenant," I announced nervously.

Lieutenant Peppel took my helmet and hollered into the mike, "Sir. . . . Yes, sir. . . . I understand, sir. It's just, she needed the plane because someone is gonna bomb the President. . . . But sir, Captain Winston . . . I believe her."

Someone else started barking questions and the lieutenant relayed what he was hearing to me. "There's some kid there with news clippings about the President's arrival in Providence. Said he saw explosives in Deputy Steyer's basement."

"That's Farley! Just ask him. He knows I'm telling the truth." Would you believe it? Farley had actually come through. Maybe it was true what Dad used to say: If you expect the best out of people, that's just what you'll get.

Lieutenant Peppel hollered, "Captain Winston. Get that FBI agent—"

"Barson," I yelled.

"Agent Barson," Lieutenant Peppel repeated. "Have him call the Providence station. Tell them to do whatever it takes, but the President's train cannot stop there." The lieutenant signed off, then told me, "They're all gonna take a car and do their best to run him down before he can reach the station. That kid Farley said his father showed him a back-road shortcut."

"There it is!" I shouted.

We dipped down out of the clouds and I spotted the plume of smoke from the President's train as it neared a small town. There were red-white-and-blue welcome banners and flags flying over the crowd that had gathered to watch the President's train pass through.

"That's the Hampton station." I checked my watch. "According to the train schedule, they're right on time."

I opened the throttle and we cleared some trees on the other side of an upcoming tunnel. But then I spotted the deputy's black-and-white Ford coupe crossing the railroad tracks up ahead, and a sick feeling came over me.

CHAPTER 18

"**A**re you sure it's the deputy's car?" the lieutenant asked.

I dipped the wing and we dove lower and pulled even with the car, five hundred feet above it. We were close enough that I could recognize the yellow Geneseo town seal on the car's black hood. I dropped even lower and buzzed the car to make sure the occupants could hear our engine. It worked. Kenji stuck his head out the passenger window. I rolled back the cockpit canopy and I waved my arms and flashed the thumbs-down bail-out signal, the one

I showed him when we were out in Father Krauss's boat. Kenji flashed it back at me. He remembered!

"It's them," I said.

"We've gotta find a way to stop him, Bird."

"But without hurting Kenji," I said.

"That's gonna make it tricky."

I glanced down in the cockpit, looking for any kind of solution. But this was a training airplane. It had no bullets and no bombs. I felt under the seat.

"We could drop the parachute?"

Lieutenant Peppel shook his head and chuckled. "With the way you fly, we might need that."

I studied the knobs and switches. I fingered the white handle on my left. It was marked FUEL.

"Could we drop a fuel tank?" I asked.

"Not without the risk of hurting Kenji. They're five hundred pounds and they'd crush the car if you hit it."

"I could always just land on the road in front of him . . . if I knew how to land."

"That car is a ton and a half of steel. This plane is made out of stressed-skin metal to be as light as it can be. That's not a fight you want to be in."

"Hey." I jiggled the red-handled lever by my right knee. "What about this?"

He grabbed hold. "Flour bombs?"

"Yeah. You knocked me flat with one, remember?" I said.

"It might work," he agreed. "But you'll have to aim it just right. You want to stop him, not make him crash. All right.

191

Climb to five hundred feet and line up a bombing run. When we start the dive, stay about ten degrees left rudder. If I remember right, that there bombsight is a little off."

"Roger," I said. I pulled the stick and we climbed toward the clouds. I took a deep breath.

"Ya ready?" he asked me.

"Okay," I said.

I dipped the nose and the mighty Warhawk picked up speed like a runaway roller-coaster car. I set my target gun-sight bead on the deputy's car. The stick began to shudder under my hand against the gravity forces pressing on the plane.

"It's okay," Lieutenant Peppel said. "She likes to buck a little. I'll keep her steady. You just line up that bull's-eye."

I squeezed my left eye and focused. We roared over the the car and—

"Bombs away!" I cried as I released the lever.

POOF! I looked down and saw the deputy's windshield caked with flour.

"Bull's-eye!" I cheered. Deputy Steyer would have to stop and pull over now.

I came around again alongside the roadster for a closer look. From my vantage point in the cockpit I saw Deputy Steyer lean out and use his hand to clear the windshield.

"Darn it. He's not slowing down," I said.

Then Kenji must have leaned over and tried to grab the wheel and make the deputy stop, because just as the car was crossing the Hampton Creek Bridge, it swerved. It careened left and then back again, into the side of the bridge, shooting sparks as its fenders scraped the railing.

"Don't crash, Kenji!" I cried out, though I knew he couldn't hear me.

"What's Kenji doing?" Lieutenant Peppel shouted.

"He grabbed the steering wheel." I hadn't planned on Kenji being so fearless that he'd risk crashing the car.

The car was zigzagging its way off the bridge when suddenly Kenji's door flew open. Deputy Steyer was leaned over, shoving Kenji by the neck. Kenji was trying to break his grip and at the same time hold on to the open door, but the deputy was too strong. With one final shove he tossed Kenji right out of the car.

"No!" I screamed.

"What happened?" the lieutenant shouted.

I dipped the wing and watched Kenji's tiny body tumble head over heels into the creek. I gave up chasing the car and tried to turn back around to find Kenji.

The lieutenant resisted my moving the stick. "Why are we turning back?"

"That dirty coward threw Kenji out of the car," I told him.

He let go of the stick and I circled the Warhawk back over the creek. But there was no sign of Kenji.

I prayed hard. *Please, God. Let him be all right. Just give him half a chance, and he'll do the rest. I know him—he's my best friend.*

A moment later something bubbled to the surface in the creek. I circled the P-40 closer.

It was Kenji.

And he was alive!

"I knew it!" It would take more than one overgrown Nazi spy to get the best of *my* best friend. I saw Kenji paddle to the shore and climb up the bank onto the bridge. When he slapped his waterlogged cowboy hat against his pant leg, I could tell he was more angry than hurt.

"I think he's okay," I said. Then I pressed the radio intercom button under my chinstrap. "Papa Bear, this is Baby Bear. Come in, Papa Bear! Captain Winston? You there?"

A moment later, Captain Winston barked into my radio earpiece, "Papa Bear? Blast it, is that you, Peppel?"

"No, sir. It's me, Bird."

"The kid?" the captain hollered. "For God's sake, who's flying that plane?"

"We both are, sir," I told him. "The lieutenant got oil in his eyes. I'm steering and working the radio."

"Criminy. Well, use your call letters, at least."

I clicked off the mike and turned to Lieutenant Peppel. "What are our call letters?"

"Baker two-six Juliet."

"This is Baker two-six Juliet. Over," I said.

"We read you, two-six Juliet. Over," the captain answered.

"Tell Agent Barson to pick up Kenji on the Hampton Creek bridge," I said. "Deputy Steyer threw him out of the car."

"That son of a—" The captain caught himself and cleared

his throat. "Ehhmm. Sorry. Roger that. I'll radio Barson. But put the lieutenant on for a moment."

I passed my helmet to the lieutenant so he could hear the captain. He listened for a few seconds.

"Roger. Yes, sir." His voice dropped low, like he'd been deflated. "Roger that. Two-six Juliet. Out." He gave me back my helmet.

"What is it? What'd Captain Winston say?"

"Bad news. There's a freight train unloading on the track ahead of the President's train. They can't get around it. The President has to stop in Providence."

"What are we gonna do?"

"Guess it's up to us to stop this thing, Peach-pit. Do you understand?"

My hands began to shake a little. "Yeah. I understand."

With the Warhawk cranked up to full throttle, we caught up with the deputy's car about ten minutes later. Below us I could see it speeding recklessly down the road. I swooped down as low as I could, right over the top of it, and pulled the bomb release.

"Take that!"

But when I looked back, the deputy's car and its windshield were clean. Somehow I'd blown it.

"I missed."

"It's not your fault." Lieutenant Peppel wiped his eyes and squinted at the car below. His vision had cleared a little. "You probably spent your load on the first drop."

"You mean we're out of ammo?"

"Guess so. We'll have to think of something else." He grabbed hold of the stick and guided us down, lower than I'd dared fly on my own, and we buzzed the deputy's car. The deputy swerved but didn't slow down. We buzzed his car a few more times, but as we neared Providence, the car disappeared beneath the trees.

We did our best to follow the road as it snaked its way through the Rhode Island landscape.

"Where is he now, Bird?" the lieutenant asked.

"He's almost to the field," I said.

Several miles ahead, the tree cover broke. I could see a clearing, and an endless sea of parked cars. From the air, they all looked an awful lot like the deputy's.

"If he gets in there, we'll lose him for sure."

Just then I caught sight of the Erie River bridge. It straddled a dry ravine up ahead, just before the clearing.

"I've got an idea," I said.

I circled the bridge and turned back to make a landing approach, coming from the opposite end toward Deputy Steyer's car.

"You're gonna try and land her? On the road? You sure you can do this?" Lieutenant Peppel hollered.

"Nope." I took a gulp of air. "But my dad was sure I could."

The road was only about as wide as the P-40's wings. The Geneseo runway was easily three or four times as wide as that. But that didn't bother me. It was the trees I was worried about. Big, green-leafed, deep-rooted oak trees lined the berm down either side, all the way to the bridge. I figured that only gave me maybe ten or fifteen feet of leeway on either side of my wingtips. This would be more like landing in a tunnel than on a runway. If I didn't land perfectly straight, if I bounced the landing or skidded off course, we'd disintegrate against those trees for sure.

I shoved the stick forward. The P-40 went into a rapid dive, head-on toward the bridge. The force of the dive flattened me against the lieutenant like a fried egg tossed against a wall. I held on, the lieutenant's hand wrapped around mine on the stick.

Suddenly my P-40's engine started to cough.

"You're stalling," the lieutenant warned.

I felt myself cry out, "Dad?" My hands shook as I struggled to control the stick and recall what Dad had told me to do.

"You've gotta dip the nose!" the lieutenant hollered. "And, uh . . ." He paused, like he was struggling to remember his flight training. "I think you increase the choke."

I turned the choke—and the plane started to sputter violently.

"No, that's not it!" I closed my eyes for an instant and tried my best to envision the manual. *In case of stall . . . increase the mixture*—I goosed it—*and dip the nose.*

I dipped her beautiful shark-mouthed nose and *PURRR!* The engine roared back to life.

"Ha-ha! I did it. I did it!" I shrieked.

"By gosh, you did, Peach-pit. Now lower your gear and give her full flaps."

I blew a huge sigh of relief, then hand-cranked down my gear and steered toward the narrow entrance to the bridge.

"Gear down. Full flaps," I echoed back.

Deputy Steyer showed no signs of stopping as he approached from the other end of the bridge. It was only going to be wide enough to fit one of us.

"How's she lining up?" asked the lieutenant.

Already I could feel that the plane was drifting. "I need left rudder!"

"Use your trim," he said. "Like you told me, remember."

I dialed the trim wheel next to my seat and my approach evened out.

"Okay. Here goes." We bounced once. I squeezed my eyes shut, anticipating the impact, and then miraculously we touched down. When I opened my eyes, tree trunks were flying past either wingtip like blurred fence posts, but I just kept focused on the bridge, straight ahead. The Warhawk's front gear bumped a few more times on the uneven highway. It felt like some wild ride in a rumble seat, but I held steady. I'd landed her.

"I did it! We're down."

"Good girl. Now throttle back, let your tail down," he said.

"I can't," I told him. "If my tail wheel drops I won't be able to see over the nose to steer."

"And he'll know you're bluffing. All right. Let's just hope he falls for it," the lieutenant said.

I kept the throttle up and barreled on toward the bridge fearlessly. I didn't bother to tell the lieutenant I had no intention of bluffing it. Only one of us—me or Deputy Steyer—was gonna make it across that bridge. Whoever flinched first would die.

The deputy barreled head-on for us, like he was dead certain we'd lose our nerve.

"You just make sure you pull up before we hit that bridge," Lieutenant Peppel said.

"Too late," I told him.

My wheels crossed onto the wooden planks of the bridge and the wingtips barely cleared the railing on either side.

"Bird!" the lieutenant cried. "What are you doing!"

"Playing chicken." If I didn't keep the plane absolutely straight, I'd shear a wing off and crash for sure.

The plane and the deputy's car were less than fifty feet apart when the deputy slammed on his brakes, finally realizing what I'd been thinking all along: It didn't matter that his car was made of steel heavier than my plane; my Warhawk's razor-sharp, twelve-foot propeller blades would cut through his car like a buzz saw.

I fought with the control stick to stay dead ahead. Lieutenant Peppel stood full-hard on the rudder pedals.

Hold her steady, I told myself.

I could just about see the smirk on the deputy's face

disappear when he flinched. He swerved his car at the last second and went crashing through the guardrail, his car flying off the bridge, tumbling and rolling into the dry riverbed a hundred feet below.

A moment after the car rolled to a stop at the bottom of the ravine, the gas tank caught fire, setting off a thunderous blast that rocked the ground beneath us. Pieces of metal blew skyward, then rained back down into the riverbed.

I taxied the P-40 to a stop and let go of the stick, exhausted.

It was maybe ten minutes later when a black Roadmaster pulled up. The passenger door slowly opened.

"Kenji!" I scrambled from the cockpit and we collided on the bridge in one big, swirling hug.

"You did it, Bird. You really did it," Kenji said.

"Yeah. We *both* did."

CHAPTER 19

In the days that followed, the frightening truth about Deputy Steyer came out. Though we had all thought he was just a regular citizen, it turned out the deputy was actually a member of something called the Abwehr, a super-secret German spy force. In the years after the First World War, hundreds of German saboteurs posing as regular immigrants were planted all over the United States. Their mission, if another war broke out, was to blow up factories and power plants, making everyone panic on the American home front, in an effort to destroy our spirit. Agent Barson said the authorities had recently caught four Nazis off Long

Island, only hours before they were set to blow up a bridge and poison the whole New York City water supply.

Here in Geneseo Bay, our own fearless Mr. Ramponi and an armada of fishermen had blockaded the inlet with their nets and managed to capture the minisubmarine, along with two more German spies. With all that had gone on, I was pretty much set for life as far as writing topics for school went.

It was a week later that the whole town was assembled around a red-white-and-blue-draped platform on the Geneseo airfield. After some words by the mayor, Agent Barson stepped onstage. He called Kenji and me to his side in front of everyone.

"It's not often we get to meet real-life heroes," he said. "But today we have two of them right here." He turned to Kenji and me. "On behalf of President Roosevelt and our country, it is my privilege to present you both with these special awards of honor."

A wave of cheering and applause drowned me and Kenji as we accepted our medals.

Then Lieutenant Peppel joined us on the stage. He bent down and pinned a pair of pilot's wings on my dress, next to my medal. Kenji tipped his new ten-gallon cowboy hat my way in salute. It was weird, but even though the country was still at war, for just a moment it seemed like all was right with the world.

It's never easy to admit you were wrong, but the folks in

town felt pretty ashamed, and they really did their best to make things right with Kenji and his uncle.

In the crowd I could see Uncle Tomo, head held high, looking proud. Margaret was showing off her new engagement ring to a circle of girlfriends. (I guess I had overdone my Cupid bit with Lieutenant Peppel.) Father Krauss caught my eye and held up a string of three good-sized catfish he'd brought to be cooked and shared. Mom looked like she was about to cry from happiness, and even that sourpuss Farley was clapping his hands.

Then a swing band struck up some Glenn Miller, people started dancing, and the real party began.

I danced a jitterbug with Kenji, ate three hot dogs, and finished off two full bottles of root beer. Then I started to feel tired, so I put my head down on the picnic table I was sitting at. It had been a long week. My eyelids got heavier and heavier.

I could still hear the music and the voices of the people, only it was like I was floating above them in a balloon. My mind was on a journey of its own, retracing all that had happened to me since my last birthday.

The war.

The spy.

The trial.

The new friend I'd found.

The old one I'd lost.

It was all like a movie newsreel at the Bijou, playing in my head. Then suddenly there was another sound. A motor. Like a car engine. Getting closer. In the distance, a shiny gold military car appeared, kicking up dust across the field. As it neared, the crowd parted and the shimmering car pulled to a stop. Slowly, a handsome soldier with one arm in a sling and a bandage around his forehead got out. Mom rushed to embrace the soldier.

It was my dad! I couldn't believe it. Margaret and Alvin covered him with hugs and kisses and the crowd went crazy.

The band was playing boogie-woogie and a squadron of P-40 Warhawks roared overhead in synchronized formation.

I watched my father and mother dance together as time seemed to slow down. Then Dad came over and took my hand.

He and I walked toward the bay. As we walked, I looked over my shoulder and saw Kenji, tearfully embraced by his mother and father. In the crowd I spotted the Widow Gorman kissing the cheek of a familiar-looking young soldier, her son, Charlie. By the refreshment stand, I caught sight of Farley telling jokes and getting his hair mussed by an older man. When the man turned around, I was shocked to see that it was Mr. Peck.

But he was dead, I told myself. And so was Charlie Gorman. And so was—

I gazed up at my father.

"Dad?"

"It's okay, Bird. Everything's gonna be okay."

We slipped away toward the shore of Geneseo Bay. There his gleaming P-40 Warhawk sat waiting. He helped me climb onto the wing, and I joined him in the cockpit. He started the engine and we took off effortlessly.

It was high summer. The air was warm and clear. You could see for miles. But as we flew, I didn't watch the sky or even the ground below. I just stared back at Dad. He looked just like I remembered him. His hair. His smile. His eyes, and the way they could always see right inside me. I looked at him a good long time.

I knew I could have shaken myself awake from that picnic table where I was sleeping. I could have woken up and joined in the party that was going on all around me. But I wasn't quite ready to shatter my perfect dream.

So I nuzzled closer, breathed him in, and smiled.

"Look." He pointed down, toward the water.

I followed the imaginary line his finger made, somewhere out toward the inlet. Then I spotted it. The Genny. Her slithery black spine broke the surface one last time, then coiled back down to the bottom and headed out to sea . . . forever.

AFTERWORD

On December 7, 1941, the Empire of Japan launched an unprovoked sneak attack on the U.S. naval base at Pearl Harbor, in Hawaii, killing 2,403 people, destroying most of the U.S. Navy, and precipitating America's entry into World War Two against the Axis Powers—Japan, Germany, and Italy. Many Americans were scared. On the West Coast of the United States, some people grew fearful that Japanese immigrants and American-born Japanese might try to help Japan sabotage, invade, and defeat the United States.

Two months after the attack on Pearl Harbor, President

Franklin D. Roosevelt signed Executive Order 9066, which forced more than 110,000 West Coast residents of Japanese ancestry to evacuate, and to sell their homes and possessions. Though these people had never shown any disloyalty or committed any crime, they were sent to live in government camps in remote desert areas of California, Colorado, Arizona, Wyoming, Arkansas, Idaho, and Utah. The camps were surrounded by barbed wire and patrolled by armed soldiers. More than two-thirds of the Japanese internees were actually American citizens, and half of them were children. Japanese residents on the East Coast were not sent to camps, since they resided outside the West Coast exclusion zone.[1]

During the Second World War, there were several attempts at sabotage made by German spies, most notably a plot to blow up bridges on the East Coast, as well as a plot to poison the water supply in New York City.[2] In June 1942 a German submarine snuck in two teams of spies off the shores of New York and Florida. All of the spies were later caught and several were executed. However, the fears and suspicions about Japanese spies in the United States proved to be unfounded. In fact, during the entire Second World War, only ten people were convicted of spying

[1] Several thousand Germans and Italians visiting or living in the United States were also detained and sent to camps, but unlike the Japanese internees, these included only non–U.S. citizens.
[2] The spies were members of the Abwehr, a true-life German spy organization that successfully planted deep-cover agents throughout the United States as early as 1925.

for Japan. None of them was Japanese; all ten were Caucasian.

In December 1944, the U.S. Supreme Court finally ruled that the detention camps violated the civil rights of interned American citizens. Over the following months in 1945, the camps were shut down and the Japanese American internees were allowed to leave. Some were angry at the way they had been treated, and after the war they chose to go to Japan. Most, however, remained in the United States and tried to rebuild their lives.

In 1988, the U.S. House of Representatives formally apologized to the Japanese internees and allocated $1.2 billion in compensation. The Civil Liberties Act of 1988 declared the evacuation and internment a grave injustice "motivated by racial prejudice, wartime hysteria, and a failure of political leadership."

When war broke out in 1941, the P-40 Warhawk was the main fighter plane of the U.S. military. By the war's end, however, it had been replaced by faster, more maneuverable planes like the P-51 Mustang, P-38 Lightning, and F4U Corsair.

Fifty years later, in 1991, the U.S. Congress lifted the female air combat ban, allowing the first American women to become combat fighter pilots.

AUTHOR'S NOTE

Some years ago I found myself at an air show in upstate New York while working on a TV series about World War Two aircraft. We were shooting a classic plane known as the Curtiss P-40 Warhawk, a rugged, very American-looking fighter with dark olive paint and a ferocious shark mouth painted on its giant conical nose. The plane had been immortalized in an old John Wayne movie, *The Flying Tigers*, and I remember feeling some childlike excitement at the chance to sit in the cockpit and be Walter Mitty for a moment while we rigged an onboard camera.

As I worked in the cockpit, two children climbed onto the

wing, admiring the historic plane. The girl was about nine or ten, with short blond hair and a defiant stare. The smart-aleck boy, who was relentlessly teasing her, was obviously her slightly older brother. They were arguing back and forth about whether the Warhawk or its sleek descendant, the P-51 Mustang, was the better plane. The girl said she didn't care what her brother said, she thought the Warhawk was the best, and one day she'd prove it by flying it.

"Girls can never be fighter pilots," he told her flatly.

I remember that his pronouncement kind of shocked her. She disputed him at first, but when he asked her to name one girl fighter pilot, of course she couldn't. She climbed down from the wing and drifted off like a deflated balloon.

Several years later, I was teaching sixth-grade English, and a female student wanted to read an action-adventure story with a girl hero. I gave it some thought, recommended a few novels, but realized none of them was really action-adventure. Some had heroines who solved mysteries, witnessed history, or survived hardships, but there were none where the girl got to save the day. By this time I was a father of two girls, and I found myself thinking more and more about that little girl at the air show. A story began to take shape in my mind.

For these reasons, and especially because a ten-year-old girl wanted to fly a P-40 Warhawk and her brother said she couldn't, I wrote *Born to Fly*.

Michael Ferrari lives in Avon Lake, Ohio, where he is a teacher. *Born to Fly* is his first novel.